Malicious Compliance

An Astoria Bay Thunder Prequel Novella

CJ Cartwright

Copper,
welcome to
the Thunder!

♡ CJ
cartwright

Emerald Fern Press

This book was made possible in part by these fabulous people:

Cover Artist: Kasmit Covers
Editor: Girls Heart Edits
Proofreader: Lunar Rose Editing Services
Formatting: Atticus

contents

PROLOGUE

Ember

10 years ago

"And we're tied, folks. The Astoria Bay Thunder against the Central City Icehawks, here in Game 5 of the Stanley Cup."

The announcer's voice booms through the packed arena, and I shiver as a rush of pure adrenaline shoots through me.

"Enjoying yourself, Ember?" My grandfather stops by my chair and smiles down at me fondly. It's impossible not to grin back at him as I meet his steely blue eyes.

To most, Hadrian Caldwell is the stony face of Caldwell Industries. A fierce competitor in the boardroom and an eccentric in his personal life. He's what some would call ridiculously rich.

Hadrian Caldwell's life is a mystery people have been determined to solve for decades. But to me, he'll always just be Gramps. He rescued me when my worthless mother took off and raised me as his own.

But here in this state-of-the-art arena nicknamed 'Olympus' - he's just another rabid hockey fan cheering for his team.

This place is our home away from home. It's far away from boardrooms and mergers and whatever the hell else he does.

Hockey is our thing. It binds us together.

I've grown up in this arena, gone to every home game, and spent countless Sunday nights having family dinners with the team. It's more than just a game for me, it's a huge part of my life.

Over the years, Caldwell Industries has spared no expense to set the Thunder up for success.

Money is no object.

New arena (partially funded by the city, but only for show). State-of-the-art training facilities. The best coaches.

In the quest for victory, the Thunder have everything they could ever dream of. But somehow, they've never quite been able to seal the deal.

Fans are packed in here shoulder to shoulder, drinks jostling and spilling. Young, old, and in-between—no one dares to breathe wrong as we watch our team edge closer and closer to the elusive victory we've never had.

We don't win things here. Some call us unlucky. Others say we're cursed.

Whatever it is, we've all learned the hard way that Astoria Bay will break your heart.

Every. Single. Time.

Something always happens.

But, like the lovestruck fools we are, we're back - season after season - hoping this year will finally be our turn.

I glance around the packed arena and smile. The crowd's enthusiasm was at a fever pitch. It's been a sweetheart of a season. The Thunder have been unstoppable, winning left and right, and the possibility of a trophy has teased our entire fanbase into a frenzy.

There's an energy in the air that speaks to all of us.

Game Five.

It's further than we have ever been.

More raucous cheering draws my attention back to the ice and the reason for the crowd's enthusiasm skating down center ice in his bright blue uniform.

Maxwell Valente.

At only 22 years old, he's one of the youngest power forwards in our league. At 6'2" and full of muscle, he's a force to be reckoned with out there. Commentators across the league whisper his name in awe. We all know we're watching a true hockey prodigy.

During one of his scouting missions a few years ago, Hadrian had found a lanky kid languishing in some high school program in the middle of nowhere and made him an offer he couldn't refuse. As soon as he graduated, Max was sent to our training team and quickly ranked up to play for the Thunder. It was his first season in the jersey, and he'd led our team to this championship playoff in one hell of a pro debut.

His skills on the ice have made h m a favorite among hockey fans, but his ice-blue eyes, long brown hair, and penchant for smoldering smirks have elevated him to a god-like status for the world at large.

The way he moves? Mmph.

There's a reason he's the guest star in dreams all over Astoria Bay, including mine.

If he pulls us through this, I can guarantee he won't ever pay for a drink in this town again... among other offers...

"MAX SPEED! MAX SPEED!" The crowd chants as Maxwell flies up the center of the ice, barreling down towards the goalposts.

I love watching him fly up the center, effortlessly moving around defenders with his eye on the prize. Power emanates from him.

"Do you think our boy will do it?" Gramps asks, appearing suddenly at my shoulder.

I can't take my eyes off the ice, and I reach for my lucky pendant and rub my thumb over it.

"Central City has the brute strength - those Vasily twins shouldn't be counted out, but Valente s fast. Unnaturally fast. I think he might," I murmur, eyes still glued to the puck.

My pulse taps giddily and I can't sit still. He's almost there.

"C'mon, you sexy fuck, shoot it in the goal!"

Three people glance over at us with amusement as my best friend Madeline presses a kiss to her hand and then smashes it down on Max's face printed on her shirt.

I grin and grab her hand.

We really, really need this win.

He lines up the shot, and it's like the entire freaking arena forgets to breathe. His form is beautiful and the ice in front of him is so clear, I swear to god it sparkles.

One more point and we take the lead.

Less than 4 minutes left in the game.

This could be it - the moment we've all been waiting for.

"Shoot it!" I pray, gripping Madeline's fist hard.

Time slows down as his stick swings back. I'm so focused on Valente's movements that I don't notice the flash of a black jersey behind him.

Until it's too late.

Impact comes just as Valente's stick touches the puck. Sticks up, the Vasily twins charge him, crashing into his sides and sandwiching him between them.

Max's helmet flies off, and the referees' whistle is barely audible over the crowd's outrage. My heart lodges in my throat when his head snaps backward on the impact, and his arms flail as he struggles to catch his balance.

The crunch of the hockey player sandwich reverberates throughout the entire arena. Tears prick my eyes.

When the Vasily twins finally push away from him and throw their sticks to the ground, Valente falls forward. The furious roar of the crowd greets them when they toss a rude gesture up at the fans.

"Get-up-get-up-get-up," I whisper. The rest of the Thunder team skates furiously to avenge their brother.

The ref forces the Icehawks back to their bench while the Thunder circle around Valente, blocking him from view.

"Oh my god, those fuckers. Did you see that hit? Is he going to be ok? Tell me, he's going to be ok, Em. We can't lose him!" Madeline is distraught. We both peer down to see what's happening on the ice.

A single tear drips down my face when the trainers and coaches motion frantically for the medics to join them.

The entire arena grows silent. Waiting.

Gramps' hand on my shoulder grounds me. Providing a steady anchor and preventing me from losing it. Even so, a profound dread permeates my soul.

"Come on, Max. You can get up," I whisper again.

The stretcher crew rolls out on the ice, and a quiet shuffle echoes through the crowd. Thunder fans and

Icehawk fans both stand in respect. Blood rushes to my ears when I stumble to my feet.

Numbly, I watch as the paramedics carefully lift Max onto the rolling stretcher. He is strapped to a spinal board, his body is unnaturally still.

"How is this happening? How could they hit him that hard?" Madeline hisses next to me, wiping her own eyes with her fist.

I don't have an answer for her. The hit was clearly illegal and designed to injure Max.

The paramedics wheel him off the ice, and the entire Thunder team skates in formation behind him.

After that, it's a blur.

Hadrian's phone rings off the hook, and hushed conversations take place all around me.

My chest is tight, and my cheeks are wet with tears.

Madeline growls a litany of profanity as she bangs on the glass of our protected box when the Vasily twins are ejected from the game.

But it doesn't matter.

I curl up into my chair and hold my knees to my chest.

The game finishes out with a victory for Central City, but I can't even muster the energy to protest or shout my anger at their ill-gotten win.

Gramps pulls me into a hug, and together, we shuffle to our private elevator. As soon as we break free from the bustle of the box, I let my tears fall.

I am crying over a hockey player who doesn't even know I exist. It makes no sense.

"He's strong, Em. Our medical team is world-class."

He tips my chin up and meets my tear-blurred gaze. I blink and manage a nod.

"Good girl. Remember this feeling - this brokenness that reminds you we're alive in this deeply flawed human race. It will fuel you later and give you valuable insight when you're the one making decisions for men you've never met."

I am lost in my grief and thoughts. When I'm the one making decisions.

The familiar lightning and cloud logo emblazoned on the elevator wall brings clarity.

He means me. And his beloved Thunder.

I chance another glance at him, and he gives me a small, knowing smile.

Making decisions for the Thunder? The thought is daunting. I grew up in this arena and hockey is basically the first love of my life but...

But...

Anxiety and determination war against each other as we step out of the elevator. Without thinking, I pull my sunglasses on and fish the ball cap out of my bag and slam it on my head. By the time we turn the corner, my strawberry blonde hair is tucked safely up under my hat, and my oversized sunglasses shield my identity as best they can.

The flash of the press cameras and clamor of reporters begging for a statement greet us as we carefully make our way to our waiting car. I'm so used to it, I move on autopilot and barely notice that Gramps isn't by my side until I am nearing the car.

Turning around in confusion, I see him standing in a knot of reporters, gesturing wildly with his arms. They press closer and I can tell he is finding his stride.

"The old man still knows how to run the press, I'll tell you that."

I face our driver, Duane, when he leans against the passenger side with me. Together, we watch as Gramps whips the mob of reporters into a frenzy.

"Do you think I'll ever be able to do what he does?" I ask softly, pulling my lucky pendant out one more time.

"Oh, girlie - Hadrian is like a tornado. He comes to town, sirens blazing and fucks shit up and leaves mayhem in his wake. But you? You're like the eye of a hurricane. Calm, collected — you'll lull them into complacency before you rock their entire world. Count on it."

For the first time since they wheeled Max off the ice, I managed a genuine smile.

"What's that necklace you're always messing with?" Duane asks me.

I open my hand to show him. Nestled against my Thunder jersey, there is a small golden charm with the number 10 on it.

He raises an eyebrow at it, and I shrug as I climb into the car.

"My birthday is August 10th."

That's enough for Duane. He's worked for Hadrian forever. Duane knows when to ask questions and when to push. When Gramps gets in the car, we speed off into the horizon.

Besides, it's not like I was lying. August 10th is my birthday.

That Maxwell Valente also has number 10? Pure coincidence. Obviously.

I look back at the twinkling lights cf the stadium, and a small smile curves my lips.

One day, the Olympus and the Thunder will be mine.

CHAPTER 1

Ember

Present

There are two types of people in this world: people who seek mindfulness to, I don't know, be a better person, and people who are ordered to find it to chill the fuck out before they're written up.

I'll let you guess which one I am.

I drop my gym bag on the floor and several of the dainty women next to me edge away.

Good. Back off, sweetheart.

The class is full of hungry women in $200 leggings, and I have never felt more out of place. When I told my assistant Gretchen to book me into some "HR-approved meditation or yoga shit," I didn't expect that she would find... this.

I eye the blonde, lime-green-clad instructor standing in the center of the airy, luxury wellness center and then glance down at my own black leggings and the ratty Thunder tank with the faded logo on it. Huh.

She keeps spraying the surrounding air with a tiny mister and exhaling loudly.

Did I hurt you somehow, Gretchen? Is this revenge? You win. You really fucking win.

I roll my eyes, slap my yoga mat on the floor, and flop down to stretch.

The woman in green removes a series of crystals from a terra cotta planter on the window, brings them over to her space, holds them over her mat, and begins chanting.

Oh boy. The next two hours are going to be really exciting.

Memo to self, find out why Gretchen is angry with you, and fix it. Whatever it takes.

"Are you calm yet, bitch?" Madeline whispers in my ear, poking me hard in the side. She slips into the spot next to me and passes me a giant water bottle.

I grab it and take a swig, which improves my mood instantly. Madeline has a unique ability to save the day with snark, alcohol, or violence. Today, she chose mimosas. Thank God.

You know what makes pretentious yoga better? Booze. It's true, Google it. Don't come at me, I don't make the rules.

The small ding of a triangle draws my attention over to our fearless... leader and I sigh.

"Welcome to this sacred space, friends. My name is Caberneigh, and I will be your guide on our journey this morning. Everyone, please gather in your spaces and we will start with some primal thoracic thrusting to open up our energies to one another." The woman in green looks out at us all expectantly.

Madeline and I are already shaking from the effort of suppressing our laughter. This does not bode well.

When a small snort escapes me, the woman next to me with the honest-to-god flower crown throws me a disgusted look.

"We're getting started, friends. I want you to reach inside yourself and harness that negative energy. Pull it out through your chest and release it to the universe—"

I raise an eyebrow when Caberneigh drops her shoulders and places her hands on her heart, pulling her palms outward before she exhales with a deep guttural noise that makes me jump and spill some mimosa down my tank.

"Holy shit! What was that?!" Madeline bursts out, stepping backward in alarm.

"Pull it out of your chest, release it - thrust it forward and let it go -" Caberneigh continues, bouncing on her feet and pulling her hand from her chest, and making deep noises on each exhale.

Slowly, the rest of the women in the room follow suit.

I look over at Madeline in horror, but she holds up her hands.

"Bitch, you're the one who got in trouble at work to warrant this - start yelling like a demon or whatever we're doing! Just think of Nils. I bet screaming will be easy."

Just the mention of his name makes me want to throw things.

Infuriating, pig-headed asshole.

Setting the mimosa bottle aside, I swing my arms to warm up and drop into the position. I close my eyes and count my breaths as I try to contain the rage simmering just below the surface.

My imagination jumps in, visualizing my rage condensed into something small and hard. Like a hockey puck.

Settling into my visualization, I imagine the puck is lined up to the goal and all I need to do is release it. I skate closer and swing my stick back. Suddenly Nils' face appears in the goal and I lose control.

"AUGHHHHHHHH," I roar as the puck crashes into his smug face.

Oddly, my chest does kind of feel lighter. Perhaps this meditation business isn't nonsense after all.

I open my eyes in triumph and swing my arms around to follow the release of the tension.

It takes me a moment to realize that the entire studio is dead silent except for a weird snuffling noise from Madeline.

The entire class is staring back at me in horror.

"Uh, did I thrust my thoracic, uh, chakra, incorrectly?" I ask, finally.

Madeline's snuffling noise grows more pronounced and I watch out of the corner of my eye as she drops to the ground in an exaggerated stretch. I think she may actually be crying.

"No, no," Caberneigh finally answers, but her voice shakes a bit. "That was excellent. Good, um, breath control. Right. Let's move on to our stretching journey, friends."

"What was that?" Madeline whispers while we stretch.

"You told me to do it! You told me to yell at Nils. I was following directions!" I hiss back, trying - and failing - to contort my body in whatever "warm up" pretzel Caberneigh is leading the class in.

"You'd tell me if you had an actual demon inside you, right?" She teased, flipping effortlessly into the next pose.

"Not since I met up with your dad-"

The ding-ding of a triangle interrupts me and I gaze up to see Caberneigh standing over us with her hands on her hips.

She looks like an angry doll.

"This space," she hisses, "is sacred. Some respect would be appropriate."

I swallow hard and purse my lips before I nod my apology.

"Perchance you can learn something from us, in the stillness," she continues, edging away from me.

"We are taking a journey today, friends. We are starting as mere tadpoles, swimming in the stream and we will emerge as beautiful frogs - singing our song on the lily pads."

I bite my lip so hard it bleeds.

"Drop to your knees, class, and prepare to receive the energy of the tadpoles."

I don't dare look at Madeline. Direct eye contact will make this whole thing go up in flames faster than you can say bullfrog.

"Find comfort on your knees, ladies. Mind your neck and make sure your posture is relaxed before you take it deeper."

Keeping silent physically hurts me, but I do my best to do what she says.

Sinking back on my heels, I kneel on my mat and roll my head back to front.

"You do not need to have your mouth open," Caberneigh says over my shoulder.

"How else am I supposed to receive the tadpole energy?" Madeline asks, innocently.

My shoulders shake from the effort of remaining silent. Perhaps this class is really a test of my self-control. If so, I'm doomed to fail.

"Once you have embodied the energy of the tadpole, lean forward and spread your legs out wider than your knees. Really lean into it and press your chest to the floor. If you can, rest your forehead on the mat."

"Good form." Caberneigh touches my shoulder and graces me with a benevolent smile.

"She's had lots of experience in the position," Madeline calls out.

Without breaking eye contact with our instructor, I reach behind me to flip Madeline the bird, but I can already feel my tenuous grip on my control slipping.

"Is there something amusing about pressing into your lily pad and emerging with the energies given to us as beautiful frogs?" Caberneigh snaps.

That does it.

That is the final straw.

The first giggle escapes me, and then all is lost. I can't undo it. Before I know it, I am face down on my mat, wheezing.

"Face down, ass up, that's the way I like to fu-" I howl.

"That's enough - get out!" Caberneigh stamps her perfect foot at us, picks up my bag, and tosses it towards the door.

"You are interjecting negative energy into our space, and I take my role as guardian of our sacred pond seriously!"

"Stop, stop, please!" Madeline cries, her face streaked with tears as she laughs, "If you keep up with the frog schtick, I'm gonna piss myself."

With great effort, Madeline and I haul ourselves out of the studio and dissolve into another round of giggles when the door slams behind us.

"Are we the bitches who just got thrown out of frog yoga?" Madeline asks, finally.

I shake my head and throw my yoga mat in the trash. "Brunch?"

By the time we're settled into a booth at our favorite diner, Madeline and I have finally regained the ability to be sane in public, mostly.

"You ok, babe?" Madeline asks me over her menu. "What the hell happened that got you sentenced to this? Everything ok with Hadrian? Did you finally stab Nils with a fork?"

I sigh heavily and take a fortifying drink of coffee before answering.

"Yes, and no. Work is... Well, it's work. It's hard being surrounded by so many great players and then having to deal with Nils. He's in the running for Asshole of the Year. I swear, I think he legitimately believes his dick gives him inside hockey knowledge. And he is always staring at me. It's creepy."

Madeline nods sympathetically.

"Gramps called me on Tuesday for lunch. Said he had big news for me and the team." I add glumly.

Just recalling the conversation sent my stomach into tight, painful coils. Madeline puts down her menu and reaches over to grab my hand.

I'm feeling desperate, and if I burst into tears, it'll just make everything worse.

"Mads, you know how hard I've worked for him. I've devoted my life to the Thunder. Two degrees, specialized training in club management. Apprenticeships, internships - more game tape than any of the coaches. Not only that, I worked my way up from the bottom. I've actively tried to learn everything there is to know about running a hockey team. It's my entire life and I know I can lead this team. They're my team."

"I know, sweets, I know. What did your granddad want?"

"To tell me that Mercer is retiring as CEO, and he's named a replacement."

"What?! Obviously, that should be you!" Madeline eyes me warily, her excitement dying as she meets my gaze. "Tell me it's you, and you're just being a drama-llama."

"It's not me," I sigh, "He won't tell me who it is at all or anything about them other than I am being reassigned to assist them."

"Like a Deputy? Or a Vice CEO? Is that a thing?"

I scoff. "Nope, according to Gramps, I'll be serving as a Special Assistant to the CEO."

Madeline's shocked gasp is oddly validating.

"What?! He's taking you out of Operations? Did he say why? Was it because you told Nils off?"

I shake my hand free from her grasp and push my hair back behind my ears.

"He says it's because I know the team better than anyone, and he wouldn't trust anyone else to help the new CEO with what needs to be done."

"I mean, at least it doesn't seem like a demotion or anything?" Madeline offers, sipping more of her coffee.

"He might not, but everyone else will. Can you imagine how insufferable Nils will be once he learns I am moving out of Hockey Ops and into the E.A. pool? Fucking prick. What's more? You rarely see people go back to Ops once they leave for Admin. It just doesn't happen."

The server comes over to take our order, but my appetite is gone. Emotions swirl through me - anger, disappointment, exhaustion, and betrayal.

No one loves the Astoria Bay Thunder more than I do.

No one.

The fact that we have an incompetent General Manager like Nils drives me absolutely batty.

"When was the last time you got laid?"

My head jerks up and I meet Madeline's twinkling eyes in surprise. "Really, Mads? Sex doesn't solve everything."

"Au contraire, mon ami. It may not solve it, but the release is good for you." She digs in her bag and pulls out a black business card with a bright purple logo on it.

"I swear to God - if that's an escort service, I'm going to stab you with a fork," I warn her before taking the card.

Madeline and I go way back. Some may call us ride or die, but that doesn't quite work for us. We're more like brunch and stab.

Flipping the card over, I see a bunch of letters and numbers jumbled together like an overly complicated password. Underneath is a tagline, "Unleash your innermost desires."

"So, my company is doing PR for this top-secret, uber-luxe dating app that caters towards the... sexually adventurous types. Just your speed. It's an invitation-only thing. They haven't officially launched yet, but I scored a few trial codes to give out at my discretion to help build buzz. Just - try it this week. Perhaps you'll connect with some Christian Grey wannabe and have yourself some kinky fuckery. It will help you work this out of your system."

I stare at the card for a long moment and then gape at her.

"Christian Grey wannabe? Really? That's who you think I go for?"

She laughs and throws a few bills on the table.

"I'm late for work but know this: We've been friends since we were six. You like the game. You love the chase. You're a kinky bitch who has turned being a pain in the ass into an art form. It's inspiring. Plus, know you'll break anyone stupid enough to think they can own you. So, yeah. Get out there, and perhaps, amid the carnage, you'll find someone who can keep up with you. You never know until you try!"

She blows me a kiss and bounces out the door, leaving me deep in thought.

She's... not wrong. I'm a contrarian by nature. I poke at rules and get a special thrill out of defiance. I love a man who can take control in the bedroom and keep up with me long enough to make me want him to take control of other aspects.

The kind that knows when to manhandle me and shove me against a wall to fuck the bratty attitude out of me and when to feed me because I'm hangry.

But those guys are few and far between.

Plus, my last name is Caldwell.

Dating as the publicly acknowledged heir of Hadrian Caldwell has contributed to some remarkably unhealthy trust issues.

I drop another bill on the table to tip the poor server who had to deal with us and pull my phone out of my bag to download the app. The design is fairly simple, and I fill out my details quickly so I can't chicken out.

Please select a username: TopShelfBrat

Describe yourself in one sentence: The eye of the storm.

What's something you wonder? Is there hockey in hell?

What are you looking for? Someone brave enough to send me to the penalty box.

Quickly, I drop a filter on a pic that partially obscures my face, upload it and close the app. My heart is pounding and my cheeks are slightly flushed from the serotonin burst of mild rebellion. Before I turn to walk back to work, the light pink paper in my purse gives me pause, and I flag down the server.

"I'll give you $100 in cash if you sign this paper for me."

The server barely glances down at my "Completion of Mandatory Course" form and scribbles her name in the box. I hand her a crisp $100 and head out into the sunshine.

Looks like this week can be saved after all. I feel calmer already.

CHaPTer 2

Max

The crack of lightning outside matches my mood.

Loud, angry, and ready for destruction.

Gone are the days where I lived comfortably out of a suitcase, always ready for the next adventure.

The next crack makes my lights flicker, and I groan. Nothing like a proper Midwestern thunderstorm to throw your entire life into question.

I pull my half-packed suitcase towards me and sigh at the amount of work left to do. The storm outside is less concerning than the storm inside my apartment. Boxes - everywhere. Chaos literally surrounds me.

My life is ruled by a sense of order and discipline. Everything has a place where it fits. Reason and logic take priority over emotions. It's been the key to my survival over the last decade. Boring? Sometimes. But it has directly led to success away from the ice.

I yawn and reach for the bottle of whiskey on my nightstand. The mouthful of alcohol burns as I swallow, and it warms my chest and grounds me to my reality.

For ten long years, I have avoided anything that reminds me of hockey. Anything that reminds me of that night.

But the mess sitting in front of me is proof that you can't avoid your past forever. Sometimes it shows up at the most unexpected moment.

"I must be out of my goddamn mind," I mutter as I wade through the mess and clear a spot at the table to sit down.

I glance down at the folder I've been avoiding and the shiny lightning bolt logo on the front.

Astoria Bay Thunder.

Just the name fills me with pain and rage and something else far more dangerous...

Hope.

I take another swig of whiskey before pulling the folder closer and swinging it open. Hadrian's letter sits on top, followed by reams of stats and player bios. My signature on the offer letter stares back at me in bright blue ink, mocking my pain with its permanence. The handwritten note scrawled across the elegant letterhead adds to my confusion and angst.

You had the skills to be great, but you have the heart of a legend. Come home and finish what you started. - Hadrian Caldwell

Redemption is a powerful draw. Hadrian Caldwell knows that more than most. When the Vasily twins charged me that night, I left more than a chance at the Cup out on that ice - I left my entire career as a pro hockey player. A chance to go back and fix that, finally win the Cup for Astoria Bay? It's as tempting as it is terrifying.

My skin crawls as the memories return like a disjointed movie playing in my mind.

The pundits and experts spent months analyzing that hit, replaying it, and discussing it from every angle. It became a part of hockey legend and lore, the kind of gruesome injury that they use in sports medicine programs as a teaching aid.

And it's in every "Greatest Hits" reel.

I never took part in the discussion. Why should I? That injury should have paralyzed me and, if it weren't for Hadrian's intervention and a metric shit ton of his money, it probably would have. He flew in the best spinal surgeon in the world for me that night and paid for all my therapies through the long months of recovery. When I said I didn't want to come back, he invested in my business and helped open some doors for me.

I am alive and successful because of Hadrian Caldwell and that, more than anything else, is why I'm headed to Astoria Bay next week...

I take another drink, hoping to stave off some of the restless energy that plagues me.

A soft knock on the door interrupts my brooding, and I haul myself up out of the chair and walk over to the door.

The tiny woman from the front desk stands in the hallway, clutching a manila envelope. She's trying valiantly not to stare at my bare chest. When another clap of thunder shakes the building, she startles and looks up at me. "Yeah?"

I step forward, filling the door frame. I wince when her eyes widen, and she instinctively takes a step back. I'm a colossal asshole.

"Uh, Mr. Valente, sir? We signed for a package while you were out... The courier was adamant that it was urgent and needed to be... attended to. Immediately."

Her voice squeaks and her cheeks flush a bright crimson red. I honestly can't tell if I scare, arouse, or annoy her.

"Thanks for bringing it up, Rosemary." I hold out my hand, and she gingerly hands me the envelope.

"You-you know my name?" she asks, still wide-eyed. She swallows reflexively and then takes a tiny step forward. "We'll sure miss having you in the building, sir."

When her soft hand touches my arm, I raise an eyebrow and look her up and down, slowly.

Arouses her. Check.

"If there's anything you need, sir. Anything I could... help you with. Just say the word. I am at your command." Her whisper is oh-so-sweet.

My dick twitches at the possibility, but I shove the urges back down and carefully untangle myself from her grip.

"Thank you for your offer, but I have no further need for your services tonight." I step back and close my door abruptly in her face.

Rosemary is a beautiful woman. Sweet, naturally submissive, with curves that could drive a man mad. She would follow my every order, seek to please me, and obey without question. I can easily imagine those doe-eyes looking up at me while her perfect pink lips wrapped themselves around my cock.

But I can never give her what she really wants. I know her type too well. She will claim she truly wants a complicated man. Maybe even swear that my idiosyncrasies, scars, and need for order doesn't scare her, but I've been down this path before.

She's been told her whole life what she should want. The whole suburban white picket fence with 2.5 kids and a dog life doesn't call to men like me. I wish it did. God, how I wish it did.

I head back into the kitchen, screw the top back on the whiskey, and shove it into an open box. Drinking myself into oblivion, while tempting, is the ultimate lack of control, and I don't have time for that.

The open folder and stacks of team information get swept into my briefcase without another glance. Some things can wait until the morning.

Methodically, I pack up my apartment until the tightness in my chest recedes. When I can breathe easily again, I pick up my phone and scan the notifications. A little alert is blinking over the purple eggplant app icon, and I roll my eyes. My friend Sheldon insisted I download a new dating app last month, and so far, it's been rough.

You have one (1) new match to review.

Sheldon swears this app is the reason for his recent whirlwind romance and subsequent bliss. It caters to a very specific clientele. With best-in-class privacy protections and an invitation-only client base, it promises to find matches for those of us with more... adventurous... tastes.

Sheldon's exact words were: "You need a person who wants what you offer. Use filters and find women who crave power exchange relationships with men in charge. Your kinks are your currency here, not a detriment. And a rich, dominant, former-pro hockey player? Yeah, you'll be fine. Plus, they guarantee privacy and discretion as much as they can."

The allure is tempting.

To only match with women looking for a submissive role in their relationship? Or know upfront that my dominant nature turns them on, rather than scares them? It takes some of the guesswork out of things. But it doesn't take away the problem that happens as soon as they google me and figure out who I am.

For once, I just want anonymity.

> TopShelfBrat. Age 25. Online now. Click "Introduce Us" to be connected to this member.

Her username makes me smile. I love the challenge of a true brat in this lifestyle. There's something about always having to be one step ahead while relishing the give and take, banter, and wild shenanigans they gravitate towards that fuels me.

It's the nature of it all. To be charged with the care of another person, to be gifted their submission, is a monumental responsibility that can be overwhelming at times. But a Brat refuses to be completely tamed. Their beauty, and allure, is in their defiance and wildness.

Intrigued, I click to read more. Her profile picture is closely cropped and heavily filtered in black and white. She's driving a Zamboni and laughing. A ball cap covers most of her hair and casts a shadow over her face. A Brat who loves hockey? What are the odds?

Her profile is sparse yet sassy. My cock stirs when I read the challenge she left for her future suitors:

What I'm looking for: Someone brave enough
to put me in the penalty box. ;)

For the first time all day, a real smile creases my face.
Game on, baby.

I click the contact tab and the chat bubble instantly
pops up.

Send a five-word greeting to TopShelfBrat.

I frown. Seriously? Five words? That's all I get? Damn.
Hardly enough to make a good first impression. I tap my
fingers against the bedspread and think. The buzz from
the whiskey makes everything slightly off-kilter.

ForwardThinking → TopShelfBrat: Don't worry,
Lucifer plays hockey.

The little message bubble turns green, showing that it
has been sent, and I stare down in horror.

Who the fuck introduces themselves by mentioning
Lucifer!? And what kind of woman responds to that? I toss
my phone on the bed in disgust. Today can fuck right off.

A cheery little ding from my phone pulls me out of my
misery.

TopShelfBrat: How are you so sure?

Well, well, well.

Either TopShelfBrat is straight-up unstable, or perhaps
she's one of the rare few who will fully appreciate my
humor.

Possibly both.

> ForwardThinking: Easy, H-E Double Hockey Sticks.

> TopShelfBrat:... Oh wow. That's... that's like a next-level dad joke. Keep that up and I'll be forced to call you Daddy. ;)

I snort and move to type a response, but another notification dings.

> TopShelfBrat requests a private chat with you. Click 'accept' to private chat with this member or 'block' if you no longer want to be connected to TopShelfBrat.

"Hell yes!" I pump my fist and click accept.

Propping myself up on my pillows, I stare down at the tiny screen in anticipation. The app blinks black before I find myself in a regular chat room. The little avatar at the bottom shows her waiting for me.

> ForwardThinking: It's not every day you meet someone searching for ways to expand the audience of winter sports to include the eternally damned. I appreciate that in a woman. Speaks well of your character.

> TopShelfBrat: Well, you know, I live to serve the Holy Order of the Puck. Thanks for noticing. How's your night going? Tell me something about yourself.

ForwardThinking: My night has been eventful. Lots of changes happening at work that take some getting used to. Nothing that time, a bottle of whiskey, and the conversation of a beautiful woman won't fix. ;)

TopShelfBrat: Ok, but... did you get thrown out of a yoga class today? Because if you did not, share your whiskey. Work woes are the worst. I send you all the zen-like energy I don't have. :)

ForwardThinking: Well, now you have to tell me that story. Oh, and call me Lee.

TopShelfBrat: Nice to meet you, Lee. You can call me Emmy. And this all started because of a certain douchebag I work with, who doesn't enjoy taking orders from owners of tits... and I have a rather magnificent set of those....

My face hurts from smiling as she regales me with the story of her shenanigans in a yoga class and the way she and her best friend interact with the world. We banter back and forth, plotting and scheming solutions to her work woes and commiserating on creative solutions to dealing with people who drive us nuts.

I almost feel guilty giving her my middle name instead of my given name, but the memories of past puck bunnies and women just looking to make a name for themselves hold me back.

By the time I put my phone down, the clock says 3:08 am. I can't remember the last time I spent 4 hours talking to anyone and enjoying it this much.

As I turn out the light and slip under the covers, one more message comes through the app. My eyes widen when I see that it's an image. I wait for the download and then squint to make it out.

It's... paint chips? I zoom in and see it's a palette of skin tone colors. Written across them in bright pink script is the word nudes.

TopShelfBrat: Think of me when you look at them. ;)

This woman may be just the one I've been waiting for.

CHAPTER 3

Ember

"You sent him an image of a paint palette and told him to think of you when he looks at them? I don't know whether to crown you Queen or ask you if you've lost your mind?" Madeline cackles as I regale her with my exploits on the drive in to work.

"He sent me a cute good morning message and gave me some suggestions on how to deal with Nils next time he pisses me off. Malicious compliance. Which, as far as good morning texts go, is probably in the Top 5 of anyone I've ever dated," I continue brightly.

Madeline just laughs. "Oh, so you're dating now? Way to lock that shit down. And malicious compliance? Do I even want to know what that means? Should I be left in the dark for legal reasons? Did you tell him who you are and who you work for?"

"Of course not. As far as he knows, my name is Emmy, and I work a nondescript corporate job with overbearing assholes. I told him about yoga, though. If he wants my name, he's going to have to put out a lot more than that. Unless you can get your PR firm to vet him for me?"

Madeline is silent for a long moment, and I hear her muffle the phone to speak with someone next to her.

"You know I can't do that. Even if I knew who he was, which I don't, the App takes privacy more seriously than anything else. But anyway, I gotta run. I have to, uh, do something."

I raise an eyebrow. Madeline sounds flustered, which is very unlike her. A deep, masculine laugh echoes in the background, followed by a high-pitched giggle.

What the puck?

"Mads, do you have a MAN at your house? And you didn't tell me? You are in so much trouble, bitch. I want details. Immediately," I threaten. "Madeline Knox, I know where you live!"

"Sorry babe, gotta run. Love you!" Madeline sounds breathless when she comes back onto the line, and then the dial tone greets me before I can respond.

She hung up on me. That bitch.

It's too hilarious for words, but it appears my bestie has been keeping secrets.

However, there's no time to contemplate a proper revenge on her for breaking the girl-code because I'm pulling into work. The first meeting on my calendar today is to discuss the operational strategy for the upcoming trade deadline.

Gretchen meets me at the door with a triple-shot macchiato because she's a goddess who keeps my life together. I don't deserve her.

"Nils is already in there, as is Mr. Caldwell and the rest of the coaching staff," she warns as I hurry down the hallway.

"What? The meeting isn't until 10! It's 9:30!" I twist my wrist to confirm the time on my watch and spill some of my precious coffee on myself.

Fucking hell.

"Nils said he wanted to do an earlier meeting and claimed he texted everyone, and they agreed. He never texted me to let me know."

Gretchen and I march down the hallway at a furious pace, making the rest of the office staff dart out of our way...

"Well, the misogynistic little asswipe forgot to text me!" I gripe.

We arrive at the boardroom door, and I toss Gretchen my jacket and purse then grab the folder she hands me and my precious coffee.

"Go get them," she mouths at me, miming a stabbing motion with her hand. I stifle a laugh and then school my features into the mildly bored expression of corporate women on the hunt for a new set of balls for our collection.

Four heads turn when I enter the room, but only Gramps looks remotely pleased to see me.

"Ember, welcome! We were just getting started. Did you get the meeting change notice early enough?" He asks solicitously.

I smile at him and move towards the chair he points to. I nod my head in greeting to each of the coaches, but when my eyes land on Nils, my gaze hardens.

"No, I must have missed that notice. Did it go through my assistant as per protocol?" I ask sweetly.

Nils sneers at me and shrugs. "I can't remember. But now that you are finally here, I suppose Mr. Caldwell will allow us to begin."

I settle back into my chair and watch Nils with polite disinterest as he launches into an exhausting monologue of his so-called vision for the team and his ideas for a 'never-been-seen-before' offense strategy that would lead us to victory.

The more excited he gets, the redder his face becomes. With his shiny bald head, he resembles a human boil, infected and ready to pop.

My phone buzzes quietly, and I glance down as discreetly as possible.

ForwardThinking: Give 'em hell today, Ms. Chaos! Make me proud.

Well, since he asked so nicely.

I scan the room and notice Gramps is watching Nils with marked displeasure. I'll never understand why he keeps the man on staff, but hopefully, this is a sign he is seeing what the rest of us see: utter incompetence.

When his phone goes off, he practically leaps out of his chair to dash out of the room and answer it. Lucky bastard.

The coaches patiently try to follow whatever he is saying about changing our offense strategy to the "egg offense."

It sounds cracked, if you ask me.

Taking inspiration from Lee, I yawn loudly. Nils zeroes in on me with another sneer.

"I don't recall asking for an executive puck bunny to discuss hockey operations. Leave, if you're so bored. Just keep your claws out of my players."

To their credit, both coaches look uncomfortable, but neither of them say anything, which is disappointing.

I just shake my head and roll my eyes.

"Oh, sorry. Is that what you were doing? Talking about hockey operations? And here I was just waiting for you to get to the fucking point and say something of substance, Nils. My apologies. I seem to have misunderstood whatever that was. Please, continue. Could you be a dear and remind me how many championships you've strategized for us? My executive puck bunny brain can't remember. Oh, is that a big giant goose... egg? Yes? Continue. It's going so well."

His face turns a particular shade of purple that is utterly fascinating as he splutters in rage. One coach covers his laugh with a cough, and I smile brighter.

Two can play this game, fuckwit.

Nils hates me.

Gretchen and I have some working theories as to why. The top one is that he tried to pick me up at the holiday party the first year he worked here, and I shot him down rather hard. But he could also just hate all women. It's honestly unclear.

Hadrian reenters the room just in time to prevent Nils from flying off the handle.

"I think that's enough for today. Nils, please wait for a call from Ember. She will handle the schedule for our incoming CEO. Ember, pencil some time in his schedule next week to meet with Nils and crew," he announces, ending the meeting, and effectively freeing us all from our prison far earlier than expected.

Nils looks like he wants to protest, but even his impressive opinion of himself won't let him contradict a direct order from the owner.

I gather my things and leave.

"Oh, Nils?" I call over my shoulder, making sure Gretchen and the rest of the admin staff are paying attention before continuing. "I'll need those loss numbers I requested by lunch today to prepare for our new leadership briefing. The new CEO deserves all the information we can give him."

I walk away and grin when I hear the crash of a chair being pushed hard into the table.

Ah, Nils. Always a pleasure.

The rest of the day passes in a blur of paperwork and preparing for the transition. Lee keeps me entertained with saucy messages at random times, and I constantly check my phone and grin like a fool.

He's a welcome distraction from the personal hell of preparing for someone else to take over the job I have worked towards for years.

It's dark by the time I drag my tired ass back out to my car and head home to the Astoria Bay Towers.

My salary isn't nearly enough to afford my apartment, but I gave up fighting Gramps on it a long time ago. He respects my need to earn my own way in the world, but the one thing he is non-negotiable on is my personal safety - and that includes my living quarters.

"The world is full of wily characters and unsavory folks. Let me protect you in this way, if nothing else, for my own peace of mind."

It's hard to argue with that kind of logic. My apartment building is the newest and tallest in Astoria Bay, with a view of the water and a secure entrance. It's entirely over-the-top for our little corner of the world, but I would be lying if I said I didn't secretly love it.

The wide open lobby, marble floors, and lush monstera plants give it a tropical hotel appearance - unusual in our cold and damp coastal climate. It's luxurious and extra and.... I love it. It's been home sweet home for the last five years.

"Good evening, Ms. Caldwell. How's the team looking this year?" George, our head of security, calls out cheerily.

"Hey, George - the Thunder are going to bring it this year! Don't you worry!" I yell back, giving him a wave.

"But is it enough to break the Valente Curse, eh?" he shouts after me.

I just shrug and shake my head.

Maxwell Valente may have only had one season in the pros, but he made one hell of an impression on the game, this town, and this team. If we're being truly honest? He made a hell of an impression on me as a person. My fingers find my tiny gold pendant, and I rub it for good luck.

I hope, wherever he is, he's found happiness. The last time I Googled him, I learned that he'd built a fortune in investments and made a name for himself as a change doctor for failing companies. He never played hockey again.

Gramps never confirmed it, but I suspect he made sure the right connections found Max in those early years, all but ensuring his overall success.

The one time I asked Gramps about him, he told me not to worry about it and changed the subject. I never asked again.

Around here? Maxwell Valente is a bonafide legend. People still talk about the hit he took, whispering theories and rehashing it a decade later. The event is baked into the collective memory of Astoria Bay.

Win or lose, and we do a lot of losing, Astoria Bay is fiercely loyal to our team. Some say the reason we haven't won a championship since that night is because justice wasn't served. Valente never got the chance to avenge his injury. Sure, the Vasily Twins were sanctioned and bounced around from team to team for a while, but that wasn't exactly justice.

Digging in my purse for my keys, I make a mental note to send George and the security team some season tickets.

Our marketing team jokes that I would give away all our tickets if it were left up to me. They're not wrong. I love this team. I love this game. I want everyone to be there to cheer our boys on.

The soft buzz of my phone sounds from my purse just as I step into the elevator.

> ForwardThinking: Evening, Chaos Demon. Tell me something. Who is your favorite hockey team?

I freeze. Telling him about the Thunder makes it all seem more... real. Real is scary. It takes our brief flirtation from online-only to the potential for offline. The thought of actually meeting Lee sends nervous butterflies to my stomach.

> TopShelfBrat: I'll tell you mine if you tell me yours.

Several minutes pass, and he doesn't reply. My stomach drops. It's been a long time since I've been this invested in an ongoing text conversation, and I have a love-hate relationship with being made to wait. Sighing, I pour myself a glass of wine.

The only reliable thing in my life is hockey.

CHAPTER 4

Max

"The situation is escalating. I need you here yesterday. If I have to sit through one more meeting and listen to Nils Knutson blather on about bullshit disguised as strategy, I will be moved to violence. Tomorrow, Max. Can you do it?"

The urgency in Hadrian's voice gives me pause.

I've never known Hadrian Caldwell to be anything but a rock wall of unflappable strength. He was a stone-cold, sometimes ruthless, decision-maker. Yet he's always had a soft spot for the Thunder. And me.

I owe Hadrian Caldwell everything.

"I'll be there by tomorrow night," I sigh, looking at the mess in my apartment with fresh eyes.

"The jet will be fueled and ready for you. I have your assistant ready to go and she will reach out with your travel information. Thank you, Max. Sincerely." Before I can respond, Hadrian hangs up. I stare at the city view with a surreal feeling.

I'm going back to Astoria Bay. Back to the Thunder.

Tomorrow. Fuck.

My emotions are so conflicted and my skin crawls in anticipation.

"Goddamn it, Max! Pull yourself together," I mutter to myself as I throw my toothbrush into the suitcase, only to dive across the table to grab it again - knocking everything to the floor.

Packing takes several hours, and it's not until I settle down on the couch to wait for the pizza I ordered that I remember Emmy.

Who I'd left hanging.

Shit.

Cringing, I open the app and am surprised to see only two messages from her. She's certainly not overly clingy.

> TopShelfBrat: Wow... you keep your hockey team close to the vest. I hope you're having a good evening.

> TopShelfBrat: I have another question for you, if you're around...

Shit.

I check the clock and see that the last message was sent over three hours ago. Poor girl probably thinks I ghosted her.

> ForwardThinking: My apologies - something at work came up, and then I had to spend some time thinking about that photo you sent last night. I'm all yours now, beautiful.

As soon as I hit send, my heart leaps into my throat. That's... creepy. I am officially a creeper. The conversation dots persist in the corner of the conversation box.

Minutes tick by.

I run a hand through my hair and exhale heavily before setting the phone down. I need a beer. I've learned from experience a text that takes this long to write is rarely good news.

Once I am adequately armed with liquid courage, I return to the couch just as the little ding indicating I have a new message goes off. A smile of relief crosses my face.

> TopShelfBrat: And here I thought you were interested in my charming personality? Just another photo hound... I get it. ;) Hopefully, work has been resolved to your satisfaction...

> TopShelfBrat: But now that I have you, I wanted to ask you about your profile. Obviously, I've studied it... at length... in the least creepy way possible. Thanks for filling it out so completely, btw. But... it says you identify as Dominant and you seek power exchange relationships. What does that mean to you?

Most women clam up and wait for me to lead the conversation as soon as they learn of my desires and preferences. Emmy clearly doesn't have that problem.

She knows what she wants, and she's willing to pursue it. Her boldness is refreshing and unusual.

Gamely, I type out my general philosophy towards power exchange. I'm nervous. I've never met this woman, never even seen her entire face. We've only been talking for a few days, yet I'm already invested. I want her to accept this side of me more than anything. It's a side that few people genuinely fully understand.

> ForwardThinking: Starting with the straightforward questions tonight? I dig it. I find myself in positions of leadership more often than not. It's where I am most comfortable, both at work and in my personal

life. It's not about the power trip and making a submissive partner obey my every arbitrary wish or any of that bullshit. It's more about the energy between us. I want to protect my partner, guide her, and help her reach her goals with discipline.

Emmy replies almost immediately.

TopShelfBrat: Well, well, well... That's refreshingly honest. Tell me about this discipline you speak of, Lee. Be detailed. Leave nothing out. Give me examples, even. Send pictorial aids. ;)

I can't help it. I actually laugh out loud. Cheeky little minx. Flirting with her makes the heavy weight on my chest lift a bit, and I am so damn grateful for it.

Forward Thinking: Oh, not so fast. Turnabout is fair play, darlin'. Your username says brat, and I want to know what that means to you. My rule is you have to start with the entrée before you get dessert. ;)

Nothing happens for a full five minutes. No conversation dots, no answer, nothing. My phone is just... blank.

What the actual fuck?

If we were in an actual relationship, I would give her a countdown before her ass was mine for leaving me hanging. But... I can't control what Emmy does right now. It's curiously infuriating and amusing at the same time.

Brats.

My phone buzzes, and I look down in surprise. A pleased smile crosses my face when I see the notification.

Incoming Call: Private Number (App Connection Services, Inc)

I answer the phone and wait for her to speak first, just to test my theory.

"I can hear you breathing, Lee. Don't tell me - you have a heavy breathing kink. I'm probably playing into it right now, aren't I? Dominant weirdo. Who doesn't answer the phone with 'hello,' or 'what,' or 'why the fuck are you calling me?'"

Her voice is warm and inviting, with just the right amount of sass.

This woman. Where has she been hiding all my life?

"Perhaps, I'm someone who was expecting a text back 5 minutes ago, not a phone call?" I retort, and then smile at her burst of laughter.

"You're the one who asked me what being a brat meant to me. There you go. Expect the unexpected. Don't be married to a specific timeline. Be ready to think on your feet. Answer your phone periodically."

I roll my eyes and make myself more comfortable on the couch. She didn't say it explicitly, but I suddenly know exactly what she's alluding to.

"Ah. Well, I prefer a certain level of order in my life. And something tells me, you do, too. You just seek it in more... chaotic ways."

I'm testing the waters of my theory.

Submissive women who identify as brats are all over the spectrum, but I have encountered quite a few successful professionals, who can't just give up control.

They need it taken from them.

"Are you calling me an agent of chaos, Lee," she giggled. "That makes me a little wet. Tell me more."

I know she's joking around. I know it. But my cock instantly reacts to her innuendo. It's been so long since I had the back-and-forth banter that we have, and I want more of it. In every way.

"I call it as I see it, babe. Besides, tell me I've got you wrong. You're a successful professional. Probably higher ranked at work than you've let on, and you have a lot of responsibility. You give orders all day long, and you expect them to be obeyed. How am I doing so far?"

She murmurs something indistinguishable, so I continue.

"But ambitious women aren't encouraged by men in this society. Some men are intimidated by it. Some men try to take you down a peg or two. Others don't even try."

She scoffs a little, but doesn't counter my argument, so I keep going, pushing my luck even further.

"Something tells me you have a strong desire to give up control sometimes, but you rarely get the opportunity to do so in a scenario that makes sense for you or is safe. You crave the high that submission gives you, but you can't turn off who you are as a person. You have an inherent need to be in control or to push back at authority, so you brat. You want the back-and-forth before you submit and to always test those boundaries before giving in when you know you're safe, because trust doesn't come easily to you."

She is silent for a beat.

"Am I wrong?"

More silence. And then I hear a sigh and rustling sound.

"Are you crazy," she asks. "Is that it? You're single because you're batshit crazy, and all your exes are in therapy because of you? Dear god, do you prefer field hockey over ice hockey? Maybe a ridiculous tattoo in homage to your ancestors on your dingaling? Something has to be wrong with you. What is it? Tell me now."

I bark out a laugh and pinch the bridge of my nose.

"Just the usual, Ms. Chaos. I work too much, don't sleep enough, and would rather watch ice hockey than anything else in the world. I can be demanding and I like things my way. No weird tattoos, kids, or unstable exes to speak of."

She inhales sharply, and I lean forward to hear her reply.

"Well, Lee, you better tell me about your hockey team now," she breathes. "Because you just read my soul and you've never even met me, and that freaks me out. Give me something here."

A warmth spreads through me at her quiet admission, and I exhale slowly.

"The Thunder. I know they aren't ever at the top of the league but, I'll be Astoria Bay until I die."

Her silence stretches longer this time, and I wish I could see her face, find out what she's doing or feeling.

"I, uh, have to go, Lee. But, talk tomorrow? Have a good night!" she says hurriedly, and then the line goes dead before I can respond.

That was... unexpected.

I replay the conversation in my head and try to identify what spooked her, but everything was fine... until I mentioned the Thunder. Weird.

Could it be that she just hates the Thunder? Hockey can be like that. Some allegiances can never be crossed. But the Thunder are pretty innocuous simply because they never, ever seem to win anymore.

My phone buzzes again, and I glance down to see an image loading notification.

> TopShelfBrat: I like you. There I said it. I'm sorry I'm so weird. I'm not good at communicating usually. But, since the Thunder's your team... maybe this will suffice as an apology for my weirdness? Good night.
> xx

The photo she sent takes my breath away. It's shot from behind, in black and white. A woman is kneeling on a wide bed facing a window, wearing an Astoria Bay Thunder hockey jersey and cheeky panties. The city lights are faintly visible through the window and her hair is up in a ponytail, sticking out of a ball cap. She looks like a fantasy come to life.

She's wearing a very familiar player jersey with the number 10 emblazoned in big numerals. My number.

My cock hardens painfully as I stare at my name written across her back. It's the sexiest thing I have ever seen.

CHAPTER 5

Ember

Lee is haunting me. That's the only explanation for my complete and utter preoccupation with a freaking stranger. I can't get him out of my head, and I'm not sure I want to.

Madeline doesn't answer when I call her, and I am forced to drive the entire way to work without processing what the hell happened last night.

He is so easy to talk to and not at all what I expected. His voice is deep and rich and his laugh sounds so genuine.

Last night, just talking about the weather with him aroused me to where I am seriously considering having him send me a voice clip reading something dirty so I can have it in the spank bank forever.

It feels foolish to say out loud, but Lee makes me feel safe.

Get it together, woman. He could still be a troll.

I still don't know what possessed me to send him my sexy Valente photo, though. A perfectly composed boudoir shot with perfect lighting and a moody black and white filter kind of sets a standard that might be impossible to maintain.

"Should have just sent him a boob pic and called it a night," I chastise myself as I walk up through the parking garage.

"You giving out tit pics now, Ms. Ember? How do I get on that list?" I whirl around, ready to embed my size 7 Louboutin heels directly into someone's ass, but I laugh when I see it's only Draven.

Draven is big, burly, and grumpy AF. Out on the ice, they call him Grave, and there are whole blogs devoted to analyzing whether he might actually kill someone out there someday. But I know better. Draven's a good guy with a rugged exterior. Sure, he's scrappy out on the ice, but in real life? He's a total cinnamon roll... not that I would ever tell him that to his face.

"Ha ha, hilarious. Tit pics are for winners, Grave. Get me the Cup and I'll consider it."

He snorts and holds the door for me. "Come down and tell the boys, Ms. Ember. That's the motivation Nils can't give us."

I chuckle and shake my head, waving him off as I ride the elevator up to the Administration offices.

Gretchen meets me at the elevator with a worried look on her face and without her clipboard. Something bad happened.

"CEO Mercer was escorted out by security 20 minutes ago," she hisses under her breath while we walk, "Mr. Caldwell's holed up in the corner office, and he's pissed. Theresa said he's throwing things into boxes and shouting on the phone." I raise my eyebrows in surprise.

"He was looking for you earlier - something about arranging travel for the new CEO to come in tonight instead of next week? I took care of it." She keeps her voice low as we walk down the hallway. "The jet has been ordered and our new mystery boss will land around 5:00 pm."

We stop before the enormous glass windows of the corner office, and sure enough, Gramps is tossing things into a big cardboard box and ranting.

"Good luck." She rests her hand on my shoulder before hurrying off. Thanks...

"Good morning?" I say as I ease into the room.

"He stole from us! Stole right from under our noses. Diverted funds from the Hockey Academy right into his own pockets," Hadrian rants. His face is bright red and his normally immaculate appearance is entirely disheveled.

My heart sinks.

We had only opened the Hockey Academy a few years ago. Designed as a partnership between the team and our local schools to inspire more kids to play hockey without financial barriers, the program has been hugely successful.

If the Thunder is Gramps' first love, then the Hockey Academy is his soul.

This is bad.

If Martin Mercer had been tampering with the Academy, he was lucky to have escaped the building with his balls intact.

No one steals from Hadrian Caldwell and lives to tell the tale. Add in stealing from underprivileged kids? Gramps will make it his personal mission to see Martin jailed and financially ruined for all time.

I awkwardly pat Gramps on the shoulder. "Gretchen tells me the new CEO is coming in tonight," I start, glancing around at the destroyed office.

He grumbles but eventually nods heavily. "Yes. He is. He's going to make some serious changes around here. Changes that are sorely needed."

"Does he have a name?" I ask lightly. The idea of another person coming in here and taking over my team rankles me. Especially when I don't even have enough information to Google him.

"He does. But you'll find out when the rest of the staff does and not before."

It takes all the limited self-control in my body to resist stomping my foot at him like a child. I hate it when he gets like this.

"Well, we better get this office back n ship-shape if the new guy is coming so soon," I chirped. I bent to rescue a spilled plant. "I am sure you have better things to do today and meetings with Legal for the Hockey Academy. I'll just... I'll take care of this."

He smiles, but it's strained. At least he's not shouting anymore.

Gramps and I walk to the door arm and arm.

"I know you're angry, Ember. But trust me on this one. It's what the team needs. Just give him a chance," he exclaims. His tired blue eyes meet mine, and he gives me a quick side hug before marching down the hallway, without even waiting to hear my response.

For the team.

Give him a chance.

Ugh.

Gramps knows just which buttons to push with me.

I press my fingers to my temple and try to count to ten, calming my heart rate enough to poke my head out the door and yell for Gretchen and the rest of the admin staff to help me fix this disaster zone.

I don't like this, but I'll give him the smallest of chances, the absolute bare minimum because Gramps asked me to. I'll be damned before I let my team fall into incompetent hands again. The only bright side to this is maybe, just maybe, we can finally get rid of Nils.

My phone buzzes, distracting me from the hell that is preparing for my replacement, and I grin when a familiar chat notification pops up.

ForwardThinking sent an image.

The team is still busy restoring the CEO's office, but I still look around the office to make sure no one is paying attention to me before opening the notification. Anticipation builds when the image takes forever to download. A part of me hopes for a spicy pic. Lee has been a gentleman, and I appreciate that, but... a little spice wouldn't go amiss.

I snort when the image finally loads. Ask and you shall receive!

His tall, muscular frame is draped across a gigantic bed. Like me, he is facing away from the camera and towards a small window. Morning light spills out through the sheer curtains, dancing over his bare, muscular back. His messy brown hair is pulled up in a man bun on top of his head. My eyes drink in the image, lingering on the tight boxer

briefs he's wearing... and the most biteable ass I have ever
seen on a man before.

My mouth actually waters, and my nipples pebble as a
rush of desire floods through me.

Yes. That. I want that. Please and thank you.

When I zoom in on his ass, I grin again. The Thunder
logo is printed along the band of his undies. I quickly save
the image and then read the message that accompanied
his thirst trap.

> ForwardThinking: Headed to Astoria Bay today
> for a work thing. Might be out of contact for a
> while on the plane. Consider this an apology
> pic, since that's what we do. Go Thunder! ;)

I read it twice.
He's coming... here?
Today? Before I chicken out, I type out a reply.

> TopShelfBrat: You're causing me to make
> inappropriate noises at work. My assistant is
> concerned about my health. So... you might
> need to apologize again. Maybe even twice.
> Once for me and once for her. #equality Or...
> we could see if you have the same effect in
> person? I live in Astoria Bay...

I don't even wait for a response. A delicious shudder of
desire rocks through me, and I can barely breathe. I never
get this worked up over a guy, and yet, something about
Lee is... intoxicating? Addicting? Mysterious? All the
above?

I'm not sure what it is, only that I want it.

"You ok, boss? You look... flushed." Gretchen grabs a
bottle of water from the mini-fridge in the CEO's office and

holds it out to me. "Drink something."

I take it and try to smile normally, but the look on her face immediately tells me how much I've failed. When my phone buzzes in my pocket, I visibly jump.

"Uh, Alison, take over. I need to go over some meeting prep with Ember," she orders before grabbing my elbow and hurrying the both of us back to our office. As soon as the door shuts between us, she turns around.

"Spill it. You're flushed and scared of your phone. What happened? Is someone threatening you? Are we trending on Twitter again? Is it McKelty?"

I love Gretchen's fierceness. She's so tiny and protective, like a mother hen.

"Uh, no, not exactly," I hedge.

I slide into my chair and rest my head on my desk.

"I met a guy," my voice is muffled, "Well, I haven't met him, met him. I just... I was talking to him and I want to bite his ass and he's not from here, but he's going to be. Here."

The words tumble out in a hurry, and I don't dare lift my head to make eye contact with Gretchen. I might die.

Her peal of laughter startles me, and I jerk upwards to watch my pitbull of an assistant absolutely lose her everloving shit. Tears stream down her face as she cackles. It's contagious. The more she laughs, the more my anxiety morphs into hilarity along with her.

Together, we laugh until our faces hurt and I am gasping for breath.

"Far be it from me to interfere with your social life, Boss, but why don't you just take the afternoon off and go... Bite his ass? You work too hard. Go have fun for once!" Gretchen finally manages in between peals of laughter.

I take big gulps of air, willing myself to calm down. When I pull my phone out, there are three unread messages from Lee.

ForwardThinking: !!! What? You live in Astoria Bay? Are you serious?

ForwardThinking: If you *are* being serious, my answer is hell yes. I'm staying at The Grand. Where do you want to meet?

ForwardThinking: Emmy! Woman, answer me! I'm boarding the plane now. Meet me in the bar at The Grand around 7. You should wear red, and I'll focus on making you make all kinds of fun noises. ;) See you soon.

I shove the phone towards Gretchen and gesture towards the messages.

"It's crazy to go meet him, right? Like, that's how I end up on some sort of unsolved crime podcast. Tell me what to do."

I'm not used to feeling this flustered. Something about Lee makes me feel extra impulsive.

Gretchen smiles and swipes through the messages he sent.

"Damn, ok. I can see why you'd want to bite that ass!" She cackles again before handing me my phone back.

"If you're worried about your safety, take a player. Make them sit in the bar and watch over you. Hell, take Draven or Kaine. They both have a soft spot for you, and god knows they can kick the ass of anyone who dares disrespect the Princess of Olympus."

Draven would give me shit for weeks, but he would do it, without question. Any of our core guys would. It would definitely provide me with a level of protection, and a built-in distraction.

"What if I just let Draven and Kaine know I am going out and ask them to be my safety check? They're both overprotective assholes when they need to be. I can share my location with them for the evening, and they can track me if anything goes sideways."

Gretchen nods thoughtfully and then pushes my phone towards me.

"Make the calls you need to, duck out early, and go buy something red..."

Logic tells you that meeting a complete stranger in their hotel bar because you like the way they make dad jokes anonymously on the internet and you want to bite their ass is.... a bad idea.

Can't say I am the biggest fan of logic these days.

There's something off-putting about stepping into the lobby of The Grand Hotel. The place isn't sleazy, per se. It's by far the nicest hotel in Astoria Bay. But, as I glance around at the men in suits and the women who are dressed up far fancier than is necessary for our little suburb, it finally clicks.

The Grand feels like a place where good suburban husbands meet their mistresses for a 'drink'.

The air reeks of intrigue, knockoff Chanel, and the overconfidence of mediocre men who cheat on their unsuspecting wives.

"Can I help you, miss?" A mustached man in a suit stops me... He's even wearing white gloves. Kill me now.

"I am meeting a friend at the bar. If you could point me in that direction, I'd appreciate it."

His eyebrows lift for a brief second before his face resumes the mask of cool professionalism. I'm pretty sure he's already assumed that I'm a call girl.

I'm a little uncomfortable with the fact that Lee and I haven't exchanged actual pictures yet. The pictures we've shared have been hot as hell, but... they are missing a key feature: our faces. Gretchen's theory is that Lee could be famous. In her mind, there is no other reason not to share pics before meeting.

If that's the case, I can't blame him. After all, that's kinda why I keep my personal info private.

Yet, here I am. Dressed to the nines in a navy blue wrap dress with a sparkly belt. I let my strawberry-blonde hair cascade down my back in soft curls and brought out my favorite berry lipstick for the occasion. My nude heels show off my fresh pedicure — steel grey on all my toes except my pinky toes.

My pinky toenails are painted a bright, fire-engine red. See, I can follow directions when I want to!

The rebellion against his perfectly reasonable request seemed exciting earlier this afternoon, but now that the moment of truth is upon me, nervous anticipation threatens to overtake me.

It's probably stupid to be this defiant to a stranger, but in my defense, he's the one who gave me so many delicious ideas and loopholes for compliance earlier. It's not my fault, it comes so naturally to me.

Besides, he specifically told me to wear red. He did not tell me where.

My phone buzzes, and I look down to see Draven and Kaine being growly via text. It makes me smile. These guys are basically my family. I've got an entire team of obnoxious brothers, and I secretly love it.

> DRAVEN: You will check in regularly, Ms. Ember. Or the boys and I are going to crash this party. Hard.

> KAINE: Don't do anything I wouldn't do. At least not without backup. ;)

Smirking, I send back a single crown emoji and take a deep breath. It's time to meet a stranger in a bar.

Here goes nothing.

CHAPTER 6

Max

What are the odds my hockey-loving chaos demon actually lives in Astoria Bay? Fate is not usually this kind to me.

Emmy has been on my mind constantly. I'm fixated on her and I know it won't end until I meet her. I wonder what she's like, and if she's as intoxicating in person as she has been through our written flirtation.

I found a booth nestled in a private corner with a direct view of the door. It keeps me out of the spotlight, on the off chance someone recognizes me, while allowing me to watch for Emmy.

When the clock on the wall finally reaches 7:00 pm, my entire body comes alive with anticipation. The bar is crowded for a Tuesday. A steady stream of people trickle in from the street, greeting each other boisterously and filling the small space.

I crane my neck to see if I can spy a flash of red in the crowd, but no one stands out to me.

A gorgeous woman in navy blue enters the room and stops a few steps away from the bar to scan the crowd. A crowd of young men bump into her and she disappears from my line of sight. Assholes.

I send off a quick message through the app, kicking myself for not at least getting Emmy's real number since we are meeting in person.

ForwardThinking: Here. Back in the booth. Black button-down shirt and man bun... I'll let you find me!

TopShelfBrat: At the bar. What are you drinking?

My gaze flies to the bar. I scrutinize each person waiting for service and try to match them to the image I have of Emmy.

There are two possibilities. The woman in navy blue who is having a very animated conversation with the bartender, or a woman in a reddish-coral power suit standing between two men and looking utterly bored.

Giving up on guessing, I watch them both and send another message.

ForwardThinking: Whiskey, neat. It's funny, I don't see a woman in red at the bar.... Is someone feeling rebellious today? ;)

The woman in blue glances down at her phone and then straightens her back and pivots in a perfect turn to scan the room again. Gotcha, baby.

I watch as she purses her lips and smirks before turning back to the bar. She grabs two drinks and wades back into the crowd.

I lose track of her again and am almost ready to get up and look for her when that charming, sassy voice sounds from right next to me.

"You know, asking a woman to meet you in a bar in downtown Astoria Bay and then have her look for a random man in a black button-down shirt does not exactly inspire confidence. You're lucky I have a sense of adventure."

She sets a glass of whiskey in front of me before sliding into the booth across from me. Her hair falls across her shoulders in gentle curls. Her dress appeared conservative from a distance, but up close, I can fully appreciate the plunging neckline.

"Eyes are up here, Lee," she teases, pointing up at her luminous brown eyes, sparkling with mischief.

"You are absolutely stunning. I can't help but look and appreciate it." I grin back. "Seriously, thank you for meeting me tonight. I know it's a risk for a woman to meet a stranger off the internet and I want to let you know I appreciate you taking the chance on me. I won't give you any reason to regret that."

I reach out and grab her smaller hand in my own and the moment my skin touches hers, a shock travels up my arm.

"Likewise," she smiles, "but speaking of risks, I need to check in with my bodyguards. They get cranky when I don't, and trust me, no one needs that drama."

Without missing a beat, she whips out her phone and takes a quick selfie with her drink and taps out a message before turning back to me.

"So. Lee. Hi. It's a pleasure to meet you. Do you like my pretty blue dress?" she asks, the picture of innocence staring back at me.

"It's beautiful - blue is one of my favorite colors. You wear it exceptionally well." I sip my drink to keep from smirking at her.

"It's very silky. It wasn't until I tried it on that I realized how versatile it is, though. After that, I had to have it," she continues, toying with the condensation on her glass before looking up at me with those big, brown eyes.

"The rule has always been, if you have a dress that looks as good on as it does in a pile on the floor... you should buy it. What kind of person would I be if I didn't follow the rules?"

The image of Emmy standing naked in my hotel room, her dress crumpled on my floor, is mind-blowing.

Point 1 goes to Emmy.

"Tell me about your day." I wave to the server and he brings over a charcuterie platter. Emmy's eyes light up, and she helps herself to some cheese and crackers.

"My day was shit. We're going through a leadership change at work and everything is tense. I don't really want to talk about that - it stresses me out. How was your day? What do you do that brings you to Astoria Bay, of all places? Did you have a pleasant flight?" She relaxes against the seat of the booth, and I try to do the same.

"I do a little of everything, but mostly investments and business consulting. I'm out here for a while doing a favor for an old friend. The flight was great - no problems, especially when I had a date to look forward to."

Her face flushes pink in pleasure, and I suddenly get the overwhelming urge to kiss her.

Conversation flows easily as we demolish the snacks in front of us. We talk about everything, except for identifying information. She tells me about her best friend, Madeline, and the trips she's been on. We discuss our shared love of the Thunder. I tell her about some of my investments and stories from my childhood.

But I stop just short of revealing my identity to her, and she doesn't ask. It's like we're both trying to skirt around information that connects us in real life.

Finally, she gives me an impish grin before draining her whiskey glass, scooting to the edge of the bench seat, and reaching for my hand.

"Lee, may I be blunt with you? I'm going to be blunt. We could spend the next two hours going back and forth in small talk, but what's the point? I don't want to talk about work. I don't want to talk about our hopes and dreams tonight. Maybe someday we can do that. Right now? I can't get you out of my head. I'm insanely attracted to you, and the way you keep looking at me, I think the feeling is mutual. So, how do you see this going tonight? Should we continue to lose our minds in the cheese and crackers, or should we lose a few hours with each other?"

Her bold words go straight to my dick, and I'm up and out of the seat before she can utter another word. I throw $100 on the table and grab her hand. Together, we stride through the bar and lobby to the elevators. Every time her eyes find mine, my heart skips a beat and my cock pulses.

We wait patiently for the doors to open and hurry inside, jamming the door-close button before anyone else can join us.

"Lee - " Emmy says something, but I can't wait any longer to taste her. I pull her in close and groan when she melts against me with a delightful little shudder. The way her breathing changes and her eyes flash with desire is mesmerizing...

"Kiss me?" she pants, moaning when I reach up to stroke her cheek with one hand.

"Since you asked so nicely," I whisper before crashing my lips to hers.

She kisses me back hungrily, pressing her body flush against mine. We're completely oblivious to anything else but each other.

A soft giggle breaks our bubble, followed by a flash of light. My head snaps up and I turn to glare at the intrusion. It's a teenage kid with his phone out and an unrepentant smirk. We've reached our floor, and I don't bother engaging with the kid.

I have much better things to do with my time tonight.

"Did that kid take a picture of us?" Emmy asks worriedly.

"He was probably just being an asshole - I wouldn't worry about it," I reassure her, quickly unlocking the door to my suite and holding it open for her.

"Wow, your boss pays for a better travel room than mine does," she calls from the living room.

"Like I said, doing a favor for a friend. It has perks!" I toss the key on the table and kick my shoes off. Hadrian insisted I take the Executive Suite, and it is way more luxurious than necessary, but tonight, I'm not complaining.

"I should say so." She runs her finger across the top of the small couch before turning to me. "I'm in your room, Lee. What ever are you going to do with me now?"

My pulse pounds hard in my throat, but I don't reach for her. Not yet.

"Tell me what you want me to do, Emmy." She bites her lip and looks down at the floor for a long moment before looking up and meeting my eyes.

"I want you to make me forget every shitty thing going on around me and just feel."

Oh, fuck yes, I can do that. "Is there anything I need to know about you to make that happen?"

She stands and carefully unhooks the sparkly little belt around her waist. As soon as it's gone, her dress falls open like a robe, and she shrugs out of it.

It pools like water at her feet, leaving her standing in my room in just her heels and a pair of bright red panties. She was right. That dress looks damn good on my floor.

Her nipples are already pebbled and her cheeks flush slightly under my gaze.

"My ass is off limits until I know you better. I don't want to be hurt or choked tonight. Not into verbal humiliation or degrading language, but depending on how everything goes, we could talk about that in the future. I think, that's it? Oh, condoms for everything."

"Mm, I can do that. Anything else?" I unbutton my shirt and fold it carefully, placing it over the edge of the couch.

"Can the first time be fast and dirty? I'm not known for my patience," she purrs, flipping her hair over her shoulder.

A wave of energy and unadulterated lust flows through me as I study her. Her soft curves and wild hair have turned her into a work of art. She stands before me with no shame or self-consciousness, and it's so fucking sexy.

I lick my lips and drag a single finger down her arm, across her breast, until I find one of her pebbled nipples. When I tweak it gently, she sways in place, leaning towards me with hooded eyes and hair mussed from our embrace in the elevator. I gently slide my palm up her neck and step forward. Her pulse is pounding beneath my hand as I stroke her cheek with my thumb. Her mouth opens ever-so-slightly, and she takes the tiniest step towards me.

I'm consumed with my need to have her, to taste her, to feel her clench around me as she comes. Her hands rest on my chest, playing in my chest hair as she waits for me to make my move.

"Come here, chaos," I whisper. I pull her roughly up against my chest, and she comes willingly, rising on her tiptoes to press a kiss to my lips, hard and fast. Her touch breaks the fragile semblance of control I had. I bury my hands in her hair and lose myself in her kisses.

Her hands drop to my waist and then lower to rub my aching cock through the outside of my jeans before slipping her hands beneath my waistband - teasing me.

We fumble together with the buttons, both laughing when I am finally free. I revel in the way her eyes widen when she sees my thick cock and the way she licks her lips, but the need to be inside her is too strong for any detours, no matter how pleasurable. With one hand, I reach for the light switch, plunging us both into darkness. With the other, I cup her ass, holding her close.

Together, we move as one, away from the couch. I back her up until her bare skin hits the cold window.

"Turn around and face the world," I growl in her ear. She turns slowly, pressing her upper body into the floor-to-ceiling window that overlooks the bay, while spreading her feet and grinding her ass against me.

"Lee, I need you," she demands, wiggling her ass at me impatiently while I fiddle with the condom packet, finally getting it open and sliding it on over my girth.

When I reach down to remove her panties, they are soaked through, and I let out a groan of appreciation.

"You are so fucking sexy," I murmur, as I slide a finger into her ready wetness. She grinds against my hand, moaning, and my control snaps.

"Brace yourself," I order, lining myself up and driving home in one powerful thrust. The weight of my thrust pushes her up against the window, pressing her face against the glass.

She gasps, and I freeze until I hear a soft giggle and feel her hips pushing back against mine.

Over and over, I drive into her, hard and deep, and she meets me, thrust for thrust. We fuck against the window, the city of Astoria Bay below us, until I feel her clench against me, her back arching up as her pussy tightens down on my cock. I bite down on her shoulder and she cries out.

The way she screams my name, squirming against me in the throes of her own climax, is enough to drive me over the edge.

I come with a roar of my own, clasping her hips to mine, pulling her hard in my last thrust.

Panting, we separate and turn to find comfort in each other's arms. I kiss her softly this time, relishing the afterglow feelings and the way she fits so perfectly in my arms. I brush her hair out of her face and look down at her.

"You are so fucking perfect, you know that?" I whisper fervently and press a kiss to her forehead.

She grins at me, her cheeks still flushed with pleasure.

"Flattery will get you everywhere. Give me a few minutes, and I'll be ready for round two! How long are you in town again?"

I laugh and slap her ass before collapsing in the nearby chair.

"Unsure at the moment, but likely a few months. I'll know more by the end of this week."

She bites her lip and gives me a soft, pleased smile. I can't remember being this happy in a long, long time. It's borderline absurd. I've always scoffed at people who say shit about soulmates, but Emmy feels... right. I need to tell her who I am.

"I stepped off the plane, dropped my bags, and headed downstairs. I need a shower before round two. Care to join me?" I ask, waggling my eyebrows at her and making her giggle.

"Sure, let me get some water first, and then I'll meet you there."

I whistle happily under my breath as I step under the warm spray. Maybe this move to Astoria Bay will be exactly what I need. Emmy certainly is.

I wait for her to join me, even sticking my head out the bathroom door to call for her, but the suite is silent.

A nervous feeling pools in my gut when I walk out into the living room, a soft towel wrapped around my waist.

Her shoes and dress are gone and my heart sinks. There's no note, no text, no sign of where she went or if she is coming back.

The only proof that she was even here is the single pair of red lace panties she left scattered on the floor.

I pick them up and look around the suite, half-hoping she might pop out in some sort of twisted surprise.

But she doesn't.

My phone dings and I dive for it, desperate to know what could have scared her off without even saying goodbye.

> TopShelfBrat: I don't enjoy being played for a fool, Maxwell. Don't contact me again.

My blood pressure skyrockets and I swear under my breath. Frantically, I look around the room for any evidence that she might have found what would have revealed my true identity, but nothing stands out to me. The documents for the Thunder are safely locked away, and my wallet is... Shit - my wallet was in my pants, which...

I backtrack into the kitchen and there, sitting open next to my discarded pants, is my slim black wallet. It lay open to my driver's license.

The half-empty water glass with the red lipstick stain is a dead giveaway.

"Damn it!" I should have told her. It's one thing to be anonymous when you're on the internet, but we have a connection. We hooked up.

She deserves to know who she hooked up with.

I pace back and forth in the living room, stopping only to stare at the smeared red lipstick on my window.

No. This doesn't end this way. She doesn't get to leave without giving me a chance to explain. We have something special, and I will fight for it.

I just need a plan.

CHAPTER 7

Ember

Lee is not Lee. He is Maxwell. Not just any Maxwell, no. He's Maxwell Valente.

Maxwell fucking Valente.

Verified hockey legend.

And he lied to me about it.

Nervous energy sparks my skin as I fumble for my keys and dash to my car in the hotel parking lot.

I don't know whether to scream, cry, or give a high five to my inner high school self for unexpectedly fulfilling one of our deepest fantasies...

It's not every day you get tricked into sleeping with the guy you spent the entirety of high school lusting over and then mourning.

It's a little surreal and my emotions are a mess.

Anger, betrayal, lust, loss, and sadness are all at war within me. Anger is the easiest to access, so I focus on that.

I tap out a quick, angry message to him through the app and hit send. The little grey button next to his name shows the option to block him and I hover over it, wavering for a moment. The memory of the photo I sent him, the one of me posing in his fucking jersey, burns through me, and I smashed my finger angrily into my phone screen.

My anger is in full swing. He had plenty of opportunities to tell me, but he chose not to. It comes down to basic level trust, and he failed with the simplest of tasks: his goddamn name. He let me humiliate myself and I can never forgive that.

My hands are shaking, and I pull out onto the main road. I don't want to go home, but I can't stand the idea of being around people.

I let Maxwell Valente fuck me against a window overlooking the entire city until I came so hard I saw stars.

The familiar blue and yellow lights of Taco Legend twinkle on my right, and I impulsively pull through the drive-thru.

A crisis of this magnitude requires three things: tacos, tequila, and a best friend. Madeline will know what to do.

Armed with my order, I drive as fast as I can to Madeline's condo. When I pull into the parking lot, another terrible thought hits me like a truck.

Max told me he was in town for work and he had to leave suddenly because something came up. A favor for an old friend. He wouldn't last long under the radar here, unless that old friend had a lot of influence. A friend like... Hadrian Caldwell.

My heart sinks even further. Surely, Gramps wouldn't spring something like that on me out of the blue. Would he?

My stomach is churning when I ring the doorbell and tears are flowing when Madeline opens the door.

"What happened?" she asks, a look of concern crossing her classically beautiful features.

I don't answer. I can't. I don't even know what to say at this point. I just push past her and stomp into her entryway. A man wearing a frilly apron and not much else steps out of the kitchen carrying a plate of waffles, and I skid to a stop. What the actual - awareness slams into me.

"Um, I'm... clearly interrupting something." I stammer. "I'll just go. I'm sorry, I didn't know..."

Madeline and her sexy chef have a whispered conversation as I slip my shoes back on.

"Babe, wait. Sheldon is going to go - you need me." Madeline pulls me into a big hug, and all the complicated emotions I have just... explode into one terrible snuffle-snort-noise.

Sheldon, to his credit, doesn't comment. He just turns his sexy ass back up the stairs and then returns, fully dressed, a few minutes later.

"You've been holding out on me," I whisper in Madeline's ear and move out of the way so they can say goodbye.

Sheldon looks at my best friend with incredible tenderness and care. It makes my chest hurt and I feel weirdly guilty watching them. He caresses her cheek, pulling her into a tight embrace before pressing a kiss on the top of her head.

"Take care of your friend, Princess. I'll call you later," he says before he kisses her and grabs his keys.

"I know we don't know each other, but let me know if there's an asshole out there that needs to meet my practice bat. I'm serious," he calls to me, miming taking a swing with a bat.

It makes me laugh and I wave at him as he leaves. The affection he and Madeline have for each other is not lost on me. I want that—more than anything.

"So. I take it your date turned out to be a troll?" Madeline hands me a waffle and opens the taco bag.

"Worse. He...." My mouth feels like cotton as I try to force the words out.

"It's Maxwell Valente. Only, he told me his name was Lee. And... I think he's who Gramps hired for the CEO position." The words pour out of me like a river, and I grab for the glass of water on the table and take a big swig.

A curious burn explodes in my chest as I gulp it and I cough - spewing it everywhere.

"Yeah, so, that's vodka," Madeline laughs, handing me a napkin to clean up and moving the offending glass to the other side of the coffee table.

"And I know I must have heard you incorrectly. Did you just say your date was Maxwell Valente?!"

I nod miserably, and Madeline's eyes get huge. "Holy shit! Why the hell are you here instead of fucking his brains out? Is he still hot? Oh, sorry, I mean... go on."

I tell her everything. The flirting, the jersey picture, the kinky discussions, the way he spoke to my soul, our meet-up, and what happened when I went back to his room. She sits there, absorbing it all and nodding.

"So, I blocked him and I'm terrified that I'm going to walk into work tomorrow and he's going to be there, and everything is going to be terrible. I know it's a double-standard because I didn't tell him my last name either, but I was honest about my first name. That's more than he can say," I finish on a wail, and Madeline pats my arm sympathetically.

"Well, the way I see it, if he is the new CEO of the Thunder, you have two options. You can just crawl under a rock, pretend it never happened, and then quietly transfer to another team to 'get experience' or something and wait it out. Or, you can get even. Do you know if he has figured out who you are yet?"

Madeline is the one you want in a crisis. She doesn't freak out, she plans. When she says get even, I know she isn't messing around.

"I don't think so? I told him to call me Emmy. And only my friends and family call me that. I'm always Ember at work. You know I won't do anything that jeopardizes the team, but... if I could make him quit, I'd be interested."

She smiles and grabs a notebook from the magazine holder next to the couch.

"Hadrian assigned you to be his assistant. Unless you want to explain why you can't work with him, we can't change that. But it's highly unlikely Hadrian will allow anyone, including Max, to fire you. Work with that. Be his assistant and sabotage him from within. Isn't he the one who told you to use malicious compliance on Nils? Maybe you could turn the tables on him and do it to him instead?"

It makes sense. My grandfather would be disappointed if I purposefully caused chaos to get my way, but there will always be a job for me with the Thunder. And, I reason, it's not like this is a tantrum for not getting the CEO position - this is revenge on a person for willfully lying to me. I'm a big enough person to recognize the benefits of having a hockey legend as a CEO, but I refuse to back down on dishonesty in my personal life.

Caldwells never forget, and we rarely forgive. If he asks, I'm just following the family motto.

"Let's do it," I decide, turning to Madeline and her ever-ready notebook.

If Maxwell Valente darkens the door of the Astoria Bay Thunder tomorrow, I'll be ready for him.

CHAPTER 8

Max

Error: Permissions to private message TopShelfBrat have been revoked.

The blinking banner stares at me from the tiny screen, a constant reminder of just how badly I fucked up. The long message that took me an hour to write last night will never be read. The strongest connection I've had in years just... severed. Over a name. Or, lack thereof.

A dark cloud hangs over my head as I make my way down to the lobby. It's foggy outside and, for once, the gloom suits my mood perfectly. The feeling of disconnect and agitation would be a bad omen for any other job, but it feels applicable to starting a position with the oft-maligned Thunder.

The hockey player cut down in his prime and the team, who never recovered. It's a match made in... hell.

Hadrian sent his personal driver to pick me up. The man points out the recent developments in the city as we cruise towards the arena, but I barely notice.

Before I'm truly ready, we're pulling up to the side entrance of Olympus and the moment I've been dreading is here.

Olympus was the gold standard for hockey arenas in the nation. Hadrian had spared no expense in building his temple for the sport, and it shows.

But the avant-garde architecture doesn't impress me. All I can remember is the last time was in this building, the night my hockey career was brutally crushed in a single instant, and I almost died in the loading bay.

"Mr. Caldwell will meet you at the entrance, Mr. Valente. And, if I may, it's good to have you home, Sir. Go Thunder!"

The driver opens my door for me, and I step out into the mist and slowly walk up the worn steps.

Two figures emerge from the mist and walk towards me, and I paste a smile on my face. No matter my inner turmoil about being back here, losing Emmy so suddenly, I have a job to do. They can say a lot of things about Maxwell Valente, but goddamn it, I'm a professional.

"Max! You made it! We're so glad to have you back," Hadrian greets me with a warm handshake, and I manage a genuine smile for him. The man never ages, he just gets more distinguished.

A young woman stands just behind him, and I move to offer her my hand.

"Hi, my name is Maxwell Valente -" I freeze. A familiar head of strawberry blonde curls snaps up and glares at me.

"Emmy?!" I gape at her. Of all the gin joints in all the world... What is she doing here?

"Ah, yes." Hadrian smiles broadly. "I promised you an assistant, and it is my absolute pleasure to introduce you to the best employee the Thunder has - my granddaughter, Ember. She will work with you to get you up to speed. Don't be afraid to use her as a resource. She has studied under every department here and is well-versed in all aspects of our operation," Hadrian continues, oblivious to the surrounding tension.

She glares at me and raises one perfectly arched eyebrow in challenge, as if daring me to admit to her grandfather that we've already met.

I narrow my eyes at her and smoothly step up to where she is perched, stepping into her personal space and offering my hand.

"It's a pleasure to meet you, Ember. I look forward to working with you."

She looks good enough to eat in her grey sweater dress. It clings in all the right places and makes me remember just how perfect her curves had felt under my hands the night before.

Hadrian's granddaughter?! Holy shit, talk about off-limits. But it's not like we can take back what we'd already done...

She narrows her eyes at me and purses her lips before offering her delicate hand to me in a limp handshake. I hold her hand much longer than necessary, enjoying the way her pulse skyrockets at my touch.

She'll never admit it, at least not right now, but she's not as unaffected by me as she wants to let on.

It gives me hope I don't deserve.

"We should show you the office, sir..."

She drops my hand and brushes her palm against her dress before pivoting smartly on her heels and marching back towards the door without waiting for us.

I gaze after her, watching the door bang shut behind her, and shake my head incredulously. That woman is pissed. But working closely together has benefits. She can at least hear me out.

Hadrian chuckles and claps my shoulder. "Don't let her prickly demeanor put you off, Max - she's a tremendous asset to the Thunder and she'll get used to you. One day, this team will be hers. She's not ready for the responsibility of command yet. You'll be good for each other, I'm sure."

Irritation prickles my skin at his words. I came back because Hadrian asked me to save our team, not to be a babysitter to a spoiled brat waiting in the wings to swoop in and take my job.

"I am sure Ms. Caldwell will be an excellent assistant. I look forward to learning about the inner workings of the operation from her." I join him on the steps, and together, we walk through the door.

Three hours as CEO of the Thunder, and I have concluded that I may have underestimated Ember Caldwell's level of pissed. I definitely underestimated her commitment to being petty.

After Hadrian introduced me around and showed me my office, he left me to get settled and promised to meet up with me after lunch.

Ember was the consummate professional in front of her grandfather - ready to assist at the drop of a hat. A competent Executive Assistant who's used to commanding a room and getting shit done.

Foolishly, I let myself think that maybe, just maybe, our professional relationship will be frosty but workable.

Yeah. No.

The second Hadrian mumbles something about lunch with the lawyers and disappears into the elevator, Ember's entire demeanor changes.

Her pleasantly neutral facial expression turns into a furious scowl, and her helpfulness changes to... hostility.

She drops an armful of folders on my desk and crosses her arms over her chest.

"If you need anything else, find it yourself. Don't like that? Leave. I'll have the jet on standby. Sir."

Before I can formulate a response, she's gone. Again. The woman is making a habit out of leaving me wrongfooted, and it's getting old.

The files she unceremoniously dropped on my desk are out of order. It takes me a full hour of sorting to realize every seventh report has been swapped into the wrong file. Accidental, I'm sure.

The office is well-appointed, at least. A larger corner space with large windows and a minibar near the seating area.

Exhaustion threatens my first full day, and I am relieved to see my personal coffee station. Eagerly, I make my coffee, adding a generous amount of sugar before sitting down to review the coaching files.

I've only taken two sips before I realize something is wrong, and I spew coffee all over my desk. Incredulously, I look down at my mug and the pool of coffee soaking the newly organized folders, and then back at the innocuous white dispenser sitting next to the creamer. Realization sits in, and I grimace.

Salt.

Not sugar.

Salt.

"Are we children here?" I grumble, looking for something to mop up my mess.

Chaos herself chooses that moment to pop into my office and survey my position with unrestrained glee.

"You have your first press interview in 10 minutes," she chirps brightly, "It looks like you have something on your shirt... try to present yourself in a manner befitting your role and the organization. We have standards here... you're a role model for the community."

My fingers flex under the desk as I try to find my inner calm.

It's difficult to remind myself that Ember is acting out because of my actions and failure to be honest with her.

But mostly, I want to spank the attitude out of her, throw her up against the wall, and fuck her twelve ways from Sunday until she can listen to reason.

I shake myself out of that diverting fantasy and earmark it for later. Ember said I had an interview in 10 minutes, and she was right - my appearance was less than my personal standards required. Coffee has already stained my white shirt and is steadily dripping onto the knee of my pants. My jacket will cover some of it, but not all of it.

Shit.

She didn't bother to tell me who the interview was with, but I have to assume the organization would have arranged for a formal press conference or maybe an exclusive with ESPN to announce the news.

Not exactly an interview I can afford to flub. There will be lots of questions about why now, why me. I need to present a unified front.

Inspiration strikes when my watch says 8 minutes left. Shit, shit, shit.

"Gretchen," I call out the door at a passing admin. Hadrian had introduced her as someone who works with Ember, but I can't remember her exact title. I can only hope Ember hasn't started a mission of turning the office staff against me... Yet.

"Yes, Mr. Valente?"

"I need a branded shirt, size large. Polo, jersey, hoodie - I don't care. But I need it in 6 minutes."

She stares at me in confusion before rolling her eyes and walking over to the cabinet near the minibar. She taps the wall, and the panel slides to the side.

"Didn't Ember show you? You have an entire closet here. We stocked it in several sizes. Surely there's something that will fit here."

Gretchen digs in one of the exposed drawers with the ruthless efficiency of a lifelong assistant, pulls out a jersey, a polo shirt, and a windbreaker, and places them on my desk.

Ember sure as shit didn't tell me about any closet. Infuriating brat.

"Take your pick, sir. By my count, you've got... Four minutes left."

Gretchen whirls out of the room as quickly as she entered. I grab the polo shirt at random and start unbuttoning my dress shirt as quickly as I can. Flinging it onto the chair, I quickly pull the polo on.

It's over my head before I realize I'm in trouble. The fit is tight over my shoulders, too tight. The fabric feels like it's holding me prisoner. I can't pull it up or down, it's wedged tightly against my shoulders. I stumble around the office, trying to wiggle my way out of the shirt, banging my knee on the corner of my desk. There's no way this is a men's large. Touche, Ember.

A flash of light followed by a low whistle and slow clapping interrupts my misery. A bevy of giggles carry in from the outer office. That answers whether my office blinds are closed. Fuck.

Nothing says "I'm here to take the organization in a new direction" like a shirtless CEO trapped in a polo shirt on his first day.

"The girls told me there was a free show up here, and they weren't kiddin'. Need a hand there, Boss?"

I whirl around to come face to face with our team captain, Levi Fawkes. His eyes are dancing with amusement. With his help, I am freed from my shirt prison and I toss the offending garment directly in the trash.

"Do I even want to know?" he asks, handing me a clean t-shirt with the Thunder logo emblazoned across it.

I double-check the tag before pulling it on.

"Fawkes, right? Walk with me. I'm late for my first interview, and my assistant disappeared without telling me where it is."

"Sure thing, Boss. Probably up on the third floor."

The team captain ambles next to me as I emerge from my office. Applause and laughter from the office staff follow us both down the hallway. A wry smile crosses my face when one of the sales assistants flushes crimson after making eye contact with me.

Revenge is sweet, Ember. So, so, sweet.

I give them all a mock bow and salute before walking with Fawkes to the elevator bay.

"So. What'd you do to piss off Ms. Ember on your first day? That takes a certain level of talent, man," he asks casually while we wait.

I studied him for a moment. "What makes you think I pissed off Ms. Caldwell?"

He smirks at me and shakes his head. "Ms. Ember is the life and soul of this club, Boss. You really believe anything happens around here without her? She's pissed at you. Everyone is talking about it."

"It's a misunderstanding. She'll calm down and then we'll have a rational conversation," I say with confidence.

Levi bursts out laughing again, "I was worried this transition was going to be difficult. I see now it's going to be entertaining as hell. I mean this sincerely, Boss. Good luck. You're going to need it."

We ride in silence while I collect my thoughts. Maybe the tight t-shirt will work for me. Show the world I'm relatable, or whatever marketing bullshit they like to say.

Ember waits for me by the elevator entrance and looks me up and down with glee. I notice her gaze lingers at my waist for a beat longer than necessary, and I wink at her.

"You're late," she snaps, gesturing with her clipboard towards an open door.

I jog towards the door and straighten my t-shirt.

On impulse, I lean in, my lips close to her ear. "Watch yourself, Emmy." She smells like citrus and sex, and I want nothing more than to kiss the pout off her face and resume what we started last night.

She straightens up and pushes away from me, scowling in annoyance.

"Or what?" She lifts her chin in challenge and points towards the room, "You'll fire me? Ha. Nope. You can't. Go to my grandfather? Good luck with that. Like it or not, you're stuck with me."

"Oh, I have no intention of getting rid of you, brat. Quite the contrary. You and I have some unfinished business to discuss."

I take a moment to enjoy the way her cheeks turn a delightful shade of red before I pivot and walk confidently into the briefing room.

Point, Valente!

Two women and five small children wait for me.

"Mr. Valente, we are the Astoria Bay Elementary School Newsletter Team," the teacher gushes. "Thank you for reaching out to allow our students to practice interviewing you. It's really quite an honor."

I glance at Ember in surprise and incline my head at her look of smug satisfaction. This should be interesting.

"On the contrary, there's no one else I would rather sit for today. I look forward to expanding the partnership the Astoria Bay Thunder has with our community and our schools. In fact, I have a gift for each of you for coming to see me today. My assistant over there is going to get you each an official Thunder t-shirt and official press passes so you can set up interviews with our players throughout the season."

The kids cheer loudly and their enthusiasm lifts the cloud of frustration I've been feeling all day long.

"Ms. Caldwell, please run along and gather our gift packs for these fine reporters," I call out dismissively, focusing entirely on my pint-sized journalists.

I'll likely need to bring my coffee for the next week or risk it all, but it's worth it. Something tells me Ember Caldwell is not used to being dismissed or ignored.

Your move, brat.

CHAPTER 9

Ember

My plan needs some adjusting. I may have underestimated my opponent.

It's been six days and the entire office is still buzzing about Max and his abs. I bite my tongue, so I don't accidentally shout something that really will get me fired. "If you think his abs are lit, wait 'til you see his dick!"

When Theresa comes up to gush about how Max is a true zaddy - I almost snap. Almost.

Any battlefield commander will tell you some battles will be lost, and that's ok. I have loftier ambitions than a mere battle - I want to win the war. Or at least the office. I have to remain strategic. Take a page out of Max's book - find the order amongst the chaos. Regroup. Strategize.

I'm playing with fire, and I know I'm going to get burned, but the temptation to keep going is just too great. I'm invested now. I have to see it through. It's petty and maybe even childish, but I don't care. It's a matter of twisted principle.

Sitting at my desk, I smile, remembering how Max looked with those kids in his press conference. I'll die before I admit to him that the way he completely focused on them and dismissed me, actually warms my heart.

He was genuinely excited to talk to them - a ragtag bunch of 5th graders that I'd pulled in at the last minute as a publicity stunt.

Thinking about it now, I feel like a bitch. If Max had turned out to be an asshole, those kids would have borne the brunt of it, and it would have been all my fault.

Bringing kids into it was a tactical error.

Operation Malicious Compliance is in full swing, but Max is proving to be resilient to my shenanigans, and I am limited by what I can in fact do to him without hurting the team.

When he asked me to order an executive calendar for him, I found one with unicorns on the cover and pink, bubblegum scented paper. He just thanked me and brought it with him when he went down to meet the girls' team at Hockey Academy. The kids loved it.

He has actually found something positive to say about every single thing I throw at him, and it's driving me nuts. I want to smack that smug look on his face when he stops by my office to thank me for being such a pain in his ass.

His compliments are so genuine, too.

It's sickening, and I need to up my game.

The high-powered business lunch appointment moved to the grocery store cafe? "Great way to improve community engagement and outreach."

The micro-business cards, printed on actual leaves? "Thinking outside the box to stand out in a sea of cards! Good work!"

Switching his ride to a client meeting from the town car service to 'Ladies' Night Party Bus'? "I think I found a new sponsor for our adult recreational league! Thanks for setting that up."

Ugh, forever.

When Max took on his persona as "Lee," he made me feel things I haven't ever felt before. He allowed me to bare my soul, talk about my deepest, darkest desires and feel safe... To find out it was all a lie is devastating.

I know he wants to talk to me, explain himself and the 'unfinished business' he claims we have, but I can't hear him out. At least not yet. He has to understand the pain he caused in his little deception if there is to be any future for us, professional or otherwise.

Madeline and I made a plan and, if I can get through it without succumbing to those scorching looks he keeps sending my way, Max Valente will rue the day he crossed me.

Gretchen rushes into my office, pulling my focus from petty revenge to more pressing matters... like hockey.

"Um, so, we're trending on Twitter," she started, wringing her hands nervously.

"Did Bridger get drunk in public again?" I prodded.

Bridger McKelty has been in and out of the news cycle for the last month following a high-profile breakup with the latest starlet-of-the-month. I sympathize with his romance woes, but his behavior in public is becoming a liability. Not that Nils or any of the coaches will do a damn thing about it.

Incompetent asswipes.

"It's you, Ember. It's a picture of you... and Max," Gretchen says softly, and I instantly go on high alert and pull my laptop towards me.

"How bad is it?" I ask as I search the trending topics for my name.

She's right, Astoria Bay Thunder is trending along with... #BossBitch and... #DoubleStandard?

That can't be right.

The picture pops up, and I gasp. It's grainy, but I am still easily identifiable. It's from a certain elevator ride, when I was wrapped around none other than Maxwell Valente in a passionate embrace. Oh shit.

"The elevator kid!" I gasp, hurriedly reading the snarky comments posted alongside the photo.

Initially, the commenters all seem amused. None that I encounter are directly abusive. My blood pressure goes down, and I take a deep breath. A kissing photo is not the end of the world. People kiss all the time. It's not insurmountable.

Out of curiosity, I click the #BossBitch tag and follow it - this time the commenters are far less kind, and the photo has been altered to include additional text.

An icy chill runs down my spine when I open the full image to see it.

The words "Executive Puck Bunny Nabs Her Hockey Has-Been Prince" have been scrawled across our kissing image in an elaborate script, and a screenshot from my dating profile has been attached, along with my profile picture. I take a deep breath and push my hair back behind my ears. My heart is hammering in my chest and a prickling feeling shoots up my spine. The phrase "executive puck bunny" niggles something in my brain, but I can't put my finger on it. I know I've heard that phrase before.

"I need IT, Hadrian, and our new CEO in a conference room in 10 minutes," I order, trying madly to ignore the rushing noise in my ears.

Gretchen nods and hurries off to gather the troops. My eyes remain glued to the computer screen. The more salacious version of the photo is racking up shares, each comment nastier than the last.

One user, IceKing696, appears to feed the fire on every post. Every comment is something about how I slept my way to the top or deride how women in leadership are ruining the sport. It makes my skin crawl.

I glance out my small window at the office, and several of my coworkers quickly look away. Great. News travels fast around here.

"You did nothing wrong. You have no reason to be ashamed. You didn't know who he was and you're both adults. Hold your head up high and go to battle," I mutter to myself as I prepare to walk the gauntlet.

Ten minutes ago, this corridor was full of giggling and boisterous conversation, but it's deathly silent as I pass by. The soft hiss of whispers, like air eaking from a balloon, follow in my wake.

I hold my head up high. Caldwells never show weakness in public.

The door to the conference room is ajar, and people are shouting. From the voices, I can tell my grandfather is already there. But Max's voice is raised too, and I stop to listen to what he is saying.

"As an organization, we will press charges and issue a statement that immediately decr es this gross invasion into the personal lives of Thunder staff. I want to be sure it pointedly reminds our community of the positive impact women have had on the world of soorts. I will not tolerate any response that implies Ember has done anything wrong. She is to be protected. End of story."

I'm surprised at the vehemence by which he defends me. It makes my heart beat a little faster, and a warmth flows from my core.

The room is packed with people, and Gretchen gives me an apologetic shrug and points towards Hadrian. Of course, he gathered the troops.

At my appearance, half a dozen voices address me at once, talking over each other and forming an incredibly outraged and supportive noise wall.

Holding my hand up for quiet, I take a deep breath and look around the room, meeting each person's eyes.

"Thank you all for coming so quickly. I know none of you planned on dealing with a privacy issue of this magnitude today."

Gramps hurries over to hug me and kisses my forehead like he did when I was a child. "We'll find the bastards, Em. I've got my best people on it."

Max catches my eye, and the look on his face resolves any tiny, lingering thoughts I might have had about him leaking the pic as revenge for my behavior. He's furious on my behalf.

His words from our whirlwind chat float randomly into my mind. "I want to protect my partner."

Max looks ready to do battle with the entire world for me.

It's a powerful feeling that I sock away in the recesses of my mind to analyze later. Maybe over tacos and tequila. For now, I have to focus on the problem at hand.

"So, damage control, what do we need to do?"

I sit in the empty chair next to Max and listen intently as they all begin bouncing ideas off each other. When his hand lands on my knee, squeezing it lightly, I don't push it off. I lean in, my shoulder just barely brushing against his.

If he wants to protect me, maybe this time, I should let him.

Without turning my head or even acknowledging him, I slide my hand under the table and squeeze his knee in return.

We have our issues, but the violation of privacy is as much his as it is mine, and neither of us asked for that.

"Ember, we have to ask. What is the nature of your relationship with Max? Is that something we can comment on? It might quiet some of the chatter."

The PR assistant looks at me nervously, and I force a smile.

"I'm his assistant. I do not have a relationship with Maxwell Valente outside of work. End of story."

Max pulls his hand away from my knee and my heart squeezes just a little at the loss of his comforting touch.

"What are our legal options?" he asks the room at large, setting off another series of discussions.

I recognize what he's trying to do, and I give him a small smile of gratitude. A small scrap of paper slides across the table from me. As discreetly as possible, I take it and unfold it.

We need to talk. Call me at this number. Please?

Hadrian rants about keyboard warriors hiding behind anonymous screens, and our PR officer cautions everyone about internet safety and optics. I just stare at the note in my hands and try to decide what to do.

A part of me wants to keep up the crusade, viewing this incident as only a setback in my overall goals. But the other part of me, the rational part, knows I owe him at least the opportunity to explain. Our ill-fated love affair being blasted all over social media kind of changes things.

My phone buzzes again, and I sigh, looking at another notification from Twitter. This time, my blood runs cold.

IceKing696 posted again. This time the image is of a car covered in spray paint and profanity, with Olympus in the background. The text accompanying the image says only two words: "Checkmate, bitch."

I slide the phone image over to Max and take a shaky breath. Fear knots in my gut and my emotions are fried. "That's my car," I whisper to him when his eyebrows shoot up in concern.

Max's foul curse brings the meeting to a complete standstill, and all eyes turn towards us.

"Get me security and the tapes from the staff parking lot. Now," he growls, slamming his palm down on the table so loud it makes Gretchen squeak in surprise.

"What happened?" Hadrian asks, looking back and forth between us.

"The troll campaign just went offline," I say tightly. "There are photos of my vehicle being vandalized here on Thunder property. Today."

None of this makes sense. I can't imagine why an image of my kissing anyone would warrant this amount of attention and threatening behavior. It's so... random.

Hadrian is almost apoplectic in his rage.

"Max - she doesn't go anywhere alone. If I'm not with her, you will be. Understood?" he snarls. "Day or night, swear it. Her safety is the most important thing."

I open my mouth to protest being treated like a child, but Max speaks before I can get a word out. "Her safety is my highest priority, sir. She will be by my side at all times."

Hadrian claps Max on the shoulder before power walking back out to the waiting security team.

What the puck just happened?! Did my grandfather just transfer custody of me to... Max?!

Suddenly, Max's protective behavior doesn't seem quite as sweet to me, and talking it out doesn't feel rational any more. It feels suffocating. Controlling.

I need to escape.

I stare at the rest of the table in outrage, waiting for someone to speak up and advocate for my autonomy. But everyone remains silent. So be it.

Calmly, I gather my things and rise to my feet, resting both hands on the tabletop and leaning forward so everyone can hear me.

"Let's make one thing clear: I will not live in fear. I don't need a babysitter. If you'll excuse me, it has been a shittastic day and I'm at my breaking point. I am going to go make a statement to the police, and then I am going home. Alone."

"Ember, you heard Hadrian. Sit down and, after the meeting, we will go to the police together," Max orders, not looking up from his phone.

The authority in his voice is clear enough to make the hair on the back of my neck stand up and my nipples twinge in anticipation.

My traitorous body hasn't gotten the memo yet that growly, Domly Max is off-limits just as much or perhaps more than Normal Level Sexy Max.

At least I'm not alone in that reaction. Several women in the room are suddenly sitting up straighter and are being very attentive to our new boss. I ignore the pang of jealousy shooting through me at the thought of him being with anyone else.

With as much calm as I can muster, I ignore his heavy-handed command and move towards the door.

"Ember! Sit down," Max tries again. This time, the warning tone is even more pronounced.

Too bad it doesn't apply to me.

I smile sweetly at him, my eyes locking in on him in pure defiance.

"Make me."

The entire conference room stills. They are watching us with undisguised interest.

The tension is so thick it makes my skin itch, but I stand my ground. Max's left eye is twitching, and I can tell he is trying to remain calm.

There is no doubt in my mind that he and I are going to talk/fight about this later. In my own twisted way, I almost look forward to it. But right now, at this moment, I can't back down. To give in would be to give up and lose the last tenuous grip I have on my sanity.

"If you'll excuse us, I need to speak with Ember alone. Please keep me apprised of the situation and any developments. I will be available via cell phone 24/7," Max says, rising from his chair in one smooth motion.

His icy blue eyes narrow on mine, and I quickly dance out of his reach and into the hall.

A thrill flows through me as I hurry through the maze of cubicles towards my private office. I genuinely wonder what he plans to do to keep me in line. Spank me? Handcuff me to his desk? Lock me in his hotel room?

A spark of heat travels immediately to my clit, and I bite my lip. I am clearly fucked up and need therapy.

"Ember!" I hear him calling after me, and I pick up the pace, making a split-second decision to hide from him.

Dashing around the corner, I dart into the emergency stairwell.

He'll catch me at some point, but the fury and fear and uncertainty that I feel won't allow me to give in until I've made him work for it. This building is my home turf.

CHAPTER 10

Max

Ember Caldwell is the most infuriating woman I have ever met. She's abrasive, vindictive, mercurial, and utterly unpredictable. Her behavior and attitude can change so quickly, you're liable to get whiplash, and she doesn't know when to back down. Her complete disregard for her personal safety is particularly concerning.

She's basically a human honey badger who spends half her time trying to kill you and the other half of the time regurgitating obscure hockey facts.

She's an oddity and possibly a liability. Yet somehow, I have never wanted to tame something more in my life. Everything about this woman seems specially designed to drive me truly insane.

From her strawberry blonde hair to her perfectly round ass - Ember Caldwell is my kryptonite. Add in that attitude, and I am basically addicted to her after a few short weeks.

It's no surprise she is making me chase that oh-so-spankable ass all the way through the building, but truthfully, I haven't felt this alive in years.

Something is bothering me about this whole picture situation. When the kid took it, I didn't get the impression that he knew who she was - just figured it was an opportunist who recognized me. It doesn't happen that often anymore, but it's not out of the ordinary either.

The coincidence between that picture and then the outing of her dating profile along with the implication that she trades sexual favors at work, screams personal attack.

I'd bet money that it's someone we both know.

The attack is just too targeted for it to be a stranger. Otherwise, why now? What would they gain from releasing a scandal like this during a leadership transition?

Theresa waves at me, and points towards the emergency stairwell, and I give her a nod of thanks. Ember's little pranks have not gone unnoticed in the office and the administrative staff are slowly picking sides. In passing, Gretchen had mentioned that there's actually a betting pool based on how far they think Ember will take it.

As long as she's safe, she can do her worst. I don't care about pink paper, stripper busses, or unicorn planners. But this casual disregard for her safety has to stop.

Loud shouts from the stairwell spur me forward, and I wrench the door open to find Ember on the landing, shaking her finger in the face of our GM, Nils, while he screams at her.

I see red.

How dare he talk to her that way!

Taking the steps two at a time, I barge in and wedge my body between Nils and Ember.

"You will meet me in my office in one hour, Nils. One hour. If you are so much as a minute late, I will assume that you no longer wish to be affiliated with this team and will take steps accordingly. Step away from Ms. Caldwell. Now."

Nils doesn't answer me. His chest is heaving and his eyes are bright. The man honestly looks deranged, and he sets off all my warning bells.

"And her?" he spits out. "Her behavior has made this team a laughingstock. Do you plan on doing anything about that, or are you just going to let that slide since you're getting it on the side?"

Ember tries to push around me with a screech of outrage, but I hip-check her hard enough to keep her from succeeding. Nils takes a step back, but he's clearly not done.

"I warned her once. Mess with my team, and the gloves come off. My team is not your personal harem. You don't get to call them up and force them to run errands for you or serve at your pleasure and then drop them. This is a professional sports team. I need my players focused."

"Your team? Your team? You don't know the first thing about hockey or our team, you incompetent, misogynistic, perverted freak! How dare you! How fucking dare you!" Ember shrieks, pelting my back with her fists to get to Nils.

Strangely, he looks gleeful at her rage. I want to punch him in his smug mouth.

"Bitches be crazy," he shrugs and walks back up the stairs. "Enjoy dealing with that, Boss. Executive puck bunnies are like cancer to a team," he calls over his shoulder before disappearing through a door.

Slowly, I turn to face Ember. She's shaking, and I can't tell if it's from fear, rage, or pain.

"Did he hurt you?" I ask cautiously. If he hurt her, Legal will need to get involved because I won't be able to stop myself from beating the shit out of the slimy dirtbag. As it stands, the Thunder are going to be shopping for a new GM tomorrow.

She shakes her head, and I let out a relieved breath.

If she's shaken, but not hurt, now would be the perfect time to talk about safety and following directions. This encounter, horrible as it was, could have been prevented if she had only listened to reason.

I refuse to imagine what could have happened if I hadn't intervened.

But the urge to talk some sense into her recedes when she turns to me and bursts into tears.

"Emmy, talk to me," I plead with her, reaching out to brush her shaking shoulders.

The simple touch only makes her cry harder, and I can tell she's in no place to have any kind of conversation right now. Fury at Nils and the mystery asshole who put her picture and info up all over the internet flows through my veins like electricity.

Something Ember said to Nils is bothering me. She called him misogynistic and perverted. My mind races as I think of all the reasons she would have to use those terms against him. None of the answers are acceptable.

She's not in a position to answer the questions I have, but I know who is. We just need to get out of the stairwell.

"Do you want to go back to your office, up to Hadrian's office, or over to mine?"

Ember wipes her eyes with the back of her sleeve and looks dejected.

"I didn't sleep with them," she says quietly, sniffling as she valiantly tries to pull herself together. "The players, I mean. They're my friends. That's all. I don't ask them to do stuff for me. I just... This team is my family. They're all I have. Gramps and the Thunder."

She shakes her head and takes a ragged breath before looking up at me sadly.

"What are you going to do about Nils?"

"I'm going to fire his ass for being verbally abusive and physically threatening to a staff member."

Her head jerks up and gratitude shines out of her chocolate brown eyes.

Without missing a beat, she launches herself at me, her lips meeting mine in a furious kiss. I can taste her tears, and I vow to make Nils suffer for the hell he's put her through. My hand skates down her back, pulling her lush body closer and deepening the kiss.

Footsteps echo above us on the stairs and she pulls away immediately, putting several steps between us as she looks guiltily at the floor. Two security guards come into view, and she reaches out to shake my hand.

Bemused, I let her.

"Thank you for checking on me, Max. I'll be in my office making a report about the car. Gretchen will be with me."

"Of course, Ember. Allow me to walk you to your door."

Together, we exit the stairwell and walk through the office in silence. She gives me a small smile when we reach the door to her office before she slips inside and locks the door.

Gretchen is hovering nearby, and I pull her aside.

"No one, except you, me, or Hadrian, goes in. If she leaves, you go with her. Understood?"

"Is she ok?" Gretchen asks me.

I nod gravely. "She's obviously shaken up, but physically, I think she's fine. I need you to tell me anything you know about any previous altercations she's had with the GM. I came across them in the middle of a screaming match."

Gretchen's expression turns guarded, and she looks around to make sure no one is listening.

"They hate each other. That part is common knowledge. But what most people don't know is that he asked her out at the holiday party a few years ago, and she turned him down. He's 40? I think? She was barely 21 and fresh out of college. He had been drinking and we think he didn't recognize her. He came onto her and started offering her tickets and such if she would go back to his office with him. After the third time, she declined and he didn't get the hint, she pulled out her ID, shoved it in his face, and told him she owned the team, so she's going to pass on, um, providing sexual acts, in exchange for tickets. Levi and Kaine and two other players overheard and got him out of there and somewhere to sober up, but he's hated her with a vengeance since then."

My face is tight with rage by the time Gretchen finishes. Nils Knutson will be done with the Astoria Bay Thunder and all of professional hockey by the time I'm through with him.

"Is there anything else you need me to know?" I ask, checking the time.

Gretchen looks around again before leaning towards me.

"I can't prove it, but I think he's the one who leaked the pics, or he knows who did. He coined a phrase for her a few years ago. "Executive puck bunny," and I haven't heard anyone else use it. He's called her that for years, and it's all over that vile post. I think it's worth looking at. Confiscate his work phone."

I grind my teeth and inhale sharply. Fucking asshole.

"Do me a favor? Get security up here and call the police. Tell them we are terminating an employee and suspect criminal activity. Then call Hadrian and tell him I'll be making some immediate personnel changes. If he would like to be present, he can meet me in my office in 15 minutes. I want the team captain there, too. Have the public relations team standing by for a statement."

Gretchen nods, jotting it all down in a little notebook. When she looks up at me, a glimmer of tears shine in her green eyes.

"Thank you for taking care of her," she says kindly.

"Keep her safe," I order, pointing at Ember's shut door before stalking back down the hallway to my corner office.

On the ice, I would have grabbed a few of my teammates and accidentally smashed this fuckwit into the glass a few times. I may not get to mete out justice like that anymore, but I'm confident I can make corporate justice hurt just as bad.

Sometimes being the boss really is the best.

"Do you want to tell me why in the hell you dragged me away from addressing an actual threat to my granddaughter to deal with some sort of personnel issue?" Hadrian huffs, marching into my office like he owns the place. Which, to be fair, he does.

"Trust me, you're going to want to be part of this," I answer tightly, pointing him to a chair off in the corner behind Levi.

He glares, but does as I ask.

Nils strolls in with one minute to spare, greeting Levi with a nod before turning to scowl at me. He crosses his arms and leans against the bookcase with a belligerent glower.

I glance through the window and catch Gretchen's signal that security has arrived. Excellent.

"Close the door, Nils," I begin. "What we need to discuss with you is sensitive and confidential."

Nils frowns at me but pushes off the bookcase to do as I requested.

I crack my knuckles in anticipation. There is a zero percent chance Nils will remain employed with the Thunder after this meeting, but the question remains if he will go to the unemployment line or jail.

The door clicks shut, and Nils turns to face the room.

"If this is about that little bitch, I don't want to hear it," he snarls. "Just because everyone else walks around here thinking her shit don't stink, doesn't mean I have to. She's a menace and an embarrassment to this organization. My team will back me up on this."

Hadrian lifts an eyebrow and turns to me. "Who is this little bitch that he is referring to?" he asks frostily.

Nils pales slightly and slams his mouth shut.

"You'd have to ask him, sir. But from the altercation I interrupted earlier, my guess would be Ms. Caldwell is the woman in question."

Hadrian leaps to his feet, his eyes blazing in fury.

"Is that true, Nils? You dare refer to my granddaughter in such a way?" His voice is dangerously calm, and Nils shifts uncomfortably on his feet. I am convinced the only reason Nils isn't fired or laid out on the floor this instant is that Hadrian trusts me to deal with this.

"Sir, I mean no disrespect to you. My responsibility is to my players, and she's a distraction, always calling them up and asking them to do things for her. It's not right," Nils whines. A slight sheen of sweat pops up on his forehead as I study him.

Levi looks distinctly uncomfortable, opening his mouth several times as if to say something before closing it again.

"Tell me, Nils, How long have you worked for the Thunder?" I ask, picking up his personnel folder and flipping through the pages with disinterest.

"Eight years," he answers quickly.

"Eight years... Interesting. Tell me, in all that time, have you ever had any complaints about you, any negative interactions with our female staff here? Other than this most recent issue with Ms. Caldwell, of course."

"Well, every now and again, some office bunny gets her feelings hurt when I tell her she can't use the players as a dating pool, but nothing more than that," he says quickly, more sweat dripping down his brow.

"I see." I let silence fill the room while I pretend to examine his file.

I already know he's lying. There are six documented complaints from junior staff over the years, alleging everything from unwanted sexual comments to verbal abuse. What doesn't make sense is why he's still working for the team? Surely Hadrian runs a tighter ship than this?

"Levi. You've been with us for eight years as well, correct?" I turn to the team captain, who is glaring at his GM.

"Yes, sir," he drawls, "Came in straight from the training team. Thunder till I die!"

"Excellent. Maybe you can shed some light on the ongoing behavior of Nils towards women? Have you ever witnessed him behave in an inappropriate or threatening manner?"

Nils pales and moves closer to the door. "This is entrapment! You can't do this! It's hearsay! Slander!" he shouts. Hadrian is practically vibrating with anger and the effort it takes to remain silent.

"Yes, sir. I have. Nils has been verbally offensive, inappropriate, and rude to just about every woman on staff, but one in particular: Ms. Ember. I would hazard a guess he hates her. The team brought several complaints to the former CEO, but it went nowhere," Levi says flatly.

Hadrian lets out a low growl and takes another step forward, but I hold my hand up to stop him. We are so close.

"I see. Thank you, Levi."

I let the silence fall in the room while I think of my next move.

The man is toast, but I wonder if I should draw it out more. Torture him like a fish on the line.

But Ember's horrified face from the stairwell flashes into my mind. Nils doesn't deserve to spend a second longer in Olympus. His presence alone is a threat to Ember and the rest of our female staff. Time to take out the trash!

"Here's what we're going to do, Nils," I begin, "An investigation is being launched, effective immediately, into these past allegations and the new ones that came to light today about your improper use of company property to take part in cyberstalking and harassment activities."

"Company property? What? You're insane." he sputters, but the blood is draining from his face as he works out what that means.

"I'll need your company phone, Nils. Your phone, tablet, and laptop," I begin, "Hand them over immediately."

"This is bullshit! Why do I have to take part in this farce? She's the one who ruins everything!"

Hadrian's self-control is dangerously thin, and I take a step towards Nils.

"Company property. On the desk. Now," I order coldly. "If you have nothing to hide, Nils, there's nothing to worry about. Is there?"

"I'll sue you for slander!" he shouts, backing away from us all.

Levi checks him into the wall and fishes his phone out of his jacket pocket.

Pinching it between two fingers, he drops it on my desk and takes several steps back.

I don't even need to unlock it to see the evidence in front of me. The bastard was so arrogant; he didn't even bother to hide it.

> IceKing696: You have thirteen (13) unread notifications.

My blood boils and I clench my fists at my side.

"Nils Knutson, upon further evidence just received, you are fired from the Astoria Bay Thunder, effective immediately. You will turn in your badge, return all Thunder property, and be escorted from the building. An investigation will be launched internally to allow for any additional victims to come forward. All evidence pertaining to your crimes will be turned over to the police."

Hadrian slaps the desk and takes two more steps towards Nils.

"And that's just the beginning, you miserable fuck. Mercer may have kept me in the dark about all this, but I'm in the light now. I'll make sure you never work in hockey again. You are never welcome on Thunder property again. Get out of my sight."

I signal Gretchen, and security comes in, wrestling Nils out while he screams about discrimination and lawsuits.

Hadrian follows them, shouting over him about how he is going to make his life hell.

Levi and I just look at each other for a long minute until finally, he extends his hand.

"Thanks for taking care of something that should have been taken care of a long time ago."

I shake his hand and nod heavily.

"It's time for some changes around here. We can't expect to win out there if we can't keep our house in order."

Levi claps me on the shoulder and shakes his head.

"You've got the team behind you. Come out with us tonight and celebrate the dawning of a new era. The Valente era!"

I laugh and follow him out the door.

For the first time in a very long time, I feel like I'm actually part of a team again. Ember's door is still closed when we pass, and I debate telling her the good news, but something tells me she needs space. With a nod to Gretchen, I scribble something on a piece of paper and hand it to her.

"For Ember, when she emerges."

It's stupid, but I need her to know. The paper only has three words on it:

Maxwell Lee Valente.

CHAPTER 11

Max

My hotel suite is cold and dark by the time I stumble in at 2:00 am. Apparently, the loss of Nils was a cause for celebration by literally everyone in the Thunder organization, but particularly the players.

Firing Nils set off a spectacular chain of events that ended in me getting drunk with the entire Thunder team and singing karaoke in Hadrian's limo. The only one missing was Ember. She showed up for a few minutes when the party started, but as soon as Xander and Kaine brought out the tequila shots, she begged off early, complaining of a headache.

Judging from the headache I already have starting, she definitely made the right choice.

Still, I miss her.

I don't even know if I have a right to, but I do. She has a way of getting under your skin and making it so you can't think, eat, breathe, or work without thinking of her.

Slowly, I stumble through the suite, undressing as I go. My shirt flies off and lands on a lamp - making me laugh out loud. My shoes thud as they hit the side of the credenza.

I reach for the buckle on my pants when I spy movement out of the corner of my eye.

"Who's there?" I call, looking around for something I can use as a weapon. The only thing available is my phone, and I hold it aloft.

The light switches on, momentarily, blinding me.

"What the hell?" I shield my eyes and glare in the intruder's direction.

Ember is sitting in my wingback chair, looking out the window.

She turns her head and slowly looks me up and down before gesturing towards the empty chair next to her.

"You're out late. Did you have fun with the boys?"

I blink and stumble into the chair.

This is weird. I could ask her how the hell she got in here, but I don't want to scare her off. The how and the why don't really matter - either way, I'm irrationally happy to see her.

Happy and drunk.

"I did. We had a lot to celebrate! They all send their love. Many promises of threats were made towards anyone who might hurt you, by the way."

She smiles at me, and my heart grows two sizes.

"Yeah... they're a great bunch of guys. The best." Her voice trails off, and she studies her nails.

My curiosity grows with each passing moment, but she remains silent.

"Did you have a good night?" I finally ask.

She shrugs and picks at a thread on the chair. "Gretchen told me you broke Nils, and he confessed everything."

"He sang like a proverbial canary," I boast. "That asshole will never bother you again. He's going to jail if the lawyers are to be believed."

"Gretchen also said you told Levi and the team they would be fired if they ever engage in cyberbullying or harassment of any kind," she continues. Her eyes are locked on mine with incredible intensity. I swallow hard.

"That's right. It's not enough that we stopped it when it happened to you. It should never have happened. We don't stand for that at the Thunder. We're better than that."

Ember sighs deeply and rises out of the chair. Her hips sway as she walks towards me, each step more hypnotic than the last.

Her dress is a deep crimson red, and she's wearing a single gold necklace with a ten on it. My pulse pounds in my head.

"Can we start over?" she whispers, stopping just in front of me.

I gape at her for a long minute, appreciating her beauty while her words settle into my drunk brain. I want this woman in whatever way I can have her. What?

"No," I burst out, startling her.

Her face falls in disappointment, and she sighs again.

"That's fair - I was a bitch to you. I should have given you a chance to explain the whole name thing. I was just... so angry and hurt. For what it's worth, Max? I'm sorry." Her admission is full of raw emotion.

My brain hurts more when she turns away and walks towards the door. Damn the entire Thunder team for getting me this drunk. I can't think of the right words!

"No! Wait!" I call after her, falling out of the chair. "I don't want to start over. I want to keep going. We both fucked up and we probably will again. Can't we just keep going?"

She pauses, giving me enough time to reach her and wrap her up in a bear hug.

Her soft gasp of surprise is music to my ears. When she softens against me, relaxing into my embrace - I know it's going to be ok. It has to be.

"Emmy. You're mine. My chaos demon. My honey badger. My sassy spitfire. I don't want to lose you," I mumble into her hair. "I want to keep you."

Her perfume, the way her body feels flush against mine, even the way her hair tickles my nose - it's all intoxicating.

I sway slightly. Drunk on her, vodka, and this moment.

"Max, let go of me." she pushes back against me, stepping out of my embrace.

"Why?" I ask stupidly.

She laughs and leans against the counter for support while she kicks off her shoes and reaches behind to unzip her dress.

I groan in approval, but she just shakes her head. Stepping out of her dress, she stands before me in a red bra and matching panties.

"You're mine, too," she whispers softly, resting her cheek on my chest. "You make me feel safe, desired, and protected. I want us to explore what we have... but I want to let it grow on its own, away from everyone else. I'm feeling selfish, Max. I want whatever this is to be just for us right now."

Just holding her is not enough to celebrate this moment - I have to taste her. Slowly, my hands skate up her arms, leaving a trail of goosebumps in their wake. I love her body. Her soft curves and silky smooth skin. I can feel her heartbeat skyrocket, but she wraps her arms around my waist and molds her body to mine.

The more I caress her, the more she squirms against me. When my lips touch the hollow of her neck, a shudder runs through her, and I grin. With my fingers buried in her hair, I hold her close and capture her lips in a blistering kiss. All the tumultuous emotions I have felt over the last few days are poured into this kiss.

By the time we pull away, both of us are breathing ragged.

"Max," she whispers, stepping back away from me. "It's 3:00 am. Take me to bed."

I nod enthusiastically, ignoring the steady pounding in my head. My fingers fumble, as I struggle to unbutton my pants.

"Damn it! Remind me to send Xander and Kaine to the fucking training team for suggesting we do shots! Those fuckwits are going to be coaching junior hockey for a month for their role in this! Levi, too, for egging them on. Bastards."

She giggles and shakes her head again, reaching for my hand.

"You're drunk, Max. And I'm exhausted. Take me to bed and let's sleep. No sex, no shenanigans, and no trading our best players while hungover. That can all wait until tomorrow."

I don't bother arguing with her - I know she's right.

"Ok, but you should know I sleep naked, and I cannot fall asleep without a goodnight kiss," I tease.

She just smiles and turns towards the bedroom. I watch her shimmy out of her panties and unhook her bra as she walks away from me.

"Come along, blue balls. I'll keep you warm. We can snuggle," she calls out over her shoulder, dropping her bra on the floor and wiggling her ass at me.

Cheeky. Little. Brat.

With a growl, I chase after her, easily capturing her and tossing her on the bed. Her shrieks of outrage soon turn to moans when I kiss her senseless.

She's pure chaos in my world of order, and I plan to spend the rest of forever chasing after her.

The End... for now.

AUTHOR'S NOTE & BONUS SCENE

Dear Reader,

Welcome to Astoria Bay, home of the Thunder! Ember and Maxwell's story is just the beginning.

Thank you so much for picking up this book and giving it a chance. Malicious Compliance was so much fun to write. Maxwell and Ember are complicated and fun.

I hope you enjoyed this introduction to my new series/world launching this fall, following an entire team of sexy hockey players and the women who love them. Need more Ember and Maxwell shenanigans? Want to find out if a certain bratty assistant gets thrown in the penalty box?

NEED THAT STEAMY PENALTY BOX SCENE? CHECK IT OUT HERE:

Enjoy this steamy penalty box bonus scene from Malicious Compliance free here: https://dl.bookfunnel.com/773q7f0082

To get all the updates on rew releases and bonus content for all things Astoria Bay and my other upcoming projects, don't forget to subscribe to my newsletter:
sendfox.com/writer.cjcartwright

Please consider leaving a review so others can find this series. Indie authors are little fish in a big pond and reviews/recommendations make a tremendous difference. Love it, hate it — I want to hear your honest review.

Did you find a typo? Ugh. Sorry about that. This book went through a lot of eyes before it got to you, but sometimes those little buggers are sneaky. Please, please don't report it to Amazon. Just send me a note at emeraldfernpress@gmail.com and I'll make sure it gets updated.

What's next? When's the next book? Are the stories going to be longer? What about the rest of the team?!

Never fear! We're headed back to Astoria Bay this fall, starting with Levi's story. Expect a full-length hockey romance novel with lots of steam, plenty of heart, and a second-chance-at-love happily ever after!
Make sure you follow my newsletter: sendfox.com/writer.cjcartwright and my Instagram page @authorcjcartwright so you know what's happening and join in the fun!
There's 15 more sexy office romances in the Men of the C-Suite collection - make sure you grab them all!

XO,
CJ

MEN OF THE C-SUITE COLLECTION

MEN OF THE C-SUITE

Men of the C-Suite is a steamy collection that features executive-level alpha males ready to sweep you off your feet (and maybe onto their desk)! If power suits and dirty talk are your thing, get ready to devour this hot new series from your favorite group of romance authors.

Made in the USA
Monee, IL
16 July 2022